The Story of th...

R. M. Ballantyn...

(1875)

C000077315

July 2013

Check out some of our other titles.
Fucking ABC's
Cursing ABC Coloring Book

Coming Soon
How I Stole 5.6 Million from Walmart

http://www.facebook.com/LokisPublishing
Seattle, WA

Chapter One.

Wreck of Winstanley's Lighthouse.

"At mischief again, of course: always at it."

Mrs Potter said this angrily, and with much emphasis, as she seized her son by the arm and dragged him out of a pool of dirty water, into which he had tumbled.

"Always at mischief of one sort or another, he is," continued Mrs Potter, with increasing wrath, "morning, noon, and night—he is; tumblin' about an' smashin' things for ever he does; he'll break my heart at last—he will. There: take that!"

"That," which poor little Tommy was desired to take, was a sounding box on the ear, accompanied by a violent shake of the arm which would have drawn that limb out of its socket if the child's bones and muscles had not been very tightly strung together.

Mrs Potter was a woman of large body and small brain. In respect of reasoning power, she was little better than the wooden cuckoo which came out periodically from the interior of the clock that stood over her own fireplace and announced the hours. She entertained settled convictions on a few subjects, in regard to which she resembled a musical box. If you set her going on any of these, she would harp away until she had played the tune out, and then begin over again; but she never varied. Reasons, however good, or facts, however weighty, were utterly powerless to penetrate her skull: her "settled convictions" were not to be unsettled by any such means. Men might change their minds; philosophers might see fit to alter their opinions; weaklings of both sexes and all ages might trim their sails in accordance with the gales of advancing knowledge, but Mrs Potter—no: never! *her* colours were nailed to the mast. Like most people who unite a strong will with an empty head, she was "wiser in her own conceit than eleven men that can render a reason:" in brief, she was obstinate.

One of her settled convictions was that her little son Tommy was "as full of mischief as a hegg is full of meat." Another of these convictions was that children of all ages are tough; that it does them good to pull them about in a violent manner, at the risk even of dislocating their joints. It mattered nothing to Mrs Potter that many of her female friends and acquaintants held a different opinion. Some of these friends suggested to her that the hearts of the poor little things were tender, as well as their muscles and bones and sinews; that children were delicate flowers, or rather buds, which required careful tending and gentle nursing. Mrs Potter's reply was invariably, "Fiddlesticks!" she knew better. They were obstinate and self-willed little brats that required constant banging. She knew how to train 'em up, she did; and it was of no manner of use, it wasn't, to talk to *her* upon that point.

She was right. It was of no use. As well might one have talked to the wooden cuckoo, already referred to, in Mrs Potter's timepiece.

"Come, Martha," said a tall, broad-shouldered, deep-voiced man at her elbow, "don't wop the poor cheeld like that. What has he been doin'—"

Mrs Potter turned to her husband with a half angry, half ashamed glance.

"Just look at 'im, John," she replied, pointing to the small culprit, who stood looking guilty and drenched with muddy water from hands to shoulders and toes to nose. "Look at 'im: see what mischief he's always gittin' into."

John, whose dress bespoke him an artisan, and whose grave earnest face betokened him a kind husband and a loving father, said:—

"Tumblin' into dirty water ain't necessarily mischief. Come, lad, speak up for yourself. How did it happen—"

"I felled into the water when I wos layin' the foundations, faither," replied the boy; pointing to a small pool, in the centre of which lay a pile of bricks.

"What sort o' foundations d'ye mean, boy?"

"The light'ouse on the Eddystun," replied the child, with sparkling eyes.

The man smiled, and looked at his son with interest.

"That's a brave boy," he said, quietly patting the child's head. "Get 'ee into th'ouse, Tommy, an' I'll show 'ee the right way to lay the foundations o' the Eddystun after supper. Come, Martha," he added, as he walked beside his wife to their dwelling near Plymouth Docks, "don't be so hard on the cheeld; it's not mischief that ails him. It's engineerin' that he's hankerin' after. Depend upon it, that if he is spared to grow up he'll be a credit to us."

Mrs Potter, being "of the same opinion still," felt inclined to say "Fiddlesticks!" but she was a good soul, although somewhat highly spiced in the temper, and respected her husband sufficiently to hold her tongue.

"John;" she said, after a short silence, "you're late to-night."

"Yes," answered John, with a sigh. "My work at the docks has come to an end, an' Mr Winstanley has got all the men he requires for the repair of the light'ouse. I saw him just before he went off to the rock to-night, an' I offered to engage, but he said he didn't want me."

"What?" exclaimed Mrs Potter, with sudden indignation: "didn't want you—you who has served 'im, off an' on, at that light'ouse for the last six year an' more while it wor a buildin'! Ah, that's gratitood, that is; that's the way some folk shows wot their consciences is made of; treats you like a pair of old shoes, they does, an' casts you off w'en you're not wanted: hah!"

Mrs Potter entered her dwelling as she spoke, and banged the door violently by way of giving emphasis to her remark.

"Don't be cross, old girl," said John, patting her shoulder: "I hope *you* won't cast me off like a pair of old shoes when you're tired of me! But, after all, I have no reason to complain. You know I have laid by a good lump of money while I was at work on the Eddystone; besides, we can't expect men to engage us when they don't require us; and if I had got employed, it would not have bin for long, being only a matter of repairs. Mr Winstanley made a strange speech, by the way, as the boat was shoving off with his men. I was standin' close by when a friend o' his came up an' said he thowt the light'ouse was in a bad way an' couldn't last long. Mr Winstanley, who is uncommon sure o' the strength of his work, he replies, says he— 'I only wish to be there in the greatest storm that ever blew under the face of heaven, to see what the effect will be.' Them's his very words, an' it did seem to me an awful wish—all the more that the sky looked at the time very like as if dirty weather was brewin' up somewhere."

"I 'ope he may 'ave 'is wish," said Mrs Potter firmly, "an' that the waves may—"

"Martha!" said John, in a solemn voice, holding up his finger, "think what you're sayin'."

"Well, I don't mean no ill; but, but—fetch the kettle, Tommy, d'ye hear? an' let alone the cat's tail, you mischievous little—"

"That's a smart boy," exclaimed John rising and catching the kettle from his son's and, just as he was on the point of tumbling over a stool: "there, now let's all have a jolly supper, and then, Tommy, I'll show you how the real foundation of the Eddystun was laid."

The building to which John Potter referred, and of which he gave a graphic account and made a careful drawing that night, for the benefit of his hopeful son, was the *first* lighthouse that was built on the wild and almost submerged reef of rocks lying about fourteen miles to the south-west of Plymouth harbour. The highest part of this reef, named the Eddystone, is only a few feet above water at high tide, and as it lies in deep water exposed to the full swell of the ocean, the raging of the sea over it in stormy weather is terrible beyond conception.

Lying as it does in the track of vessels coasting up and down the English Channel, it was, as we may easily believe, a source of terror, as well as of danger, to mariners, until a lighthouse was built upon it.

But a lighthouse was talked of long before any attempt was made to erect one. Important though this object was to the navies of the world, the supposed impossibility of the feat, and the danger apprehended in the mere attempt, deterred any one from undertaking the task until the year 1696, when a country gentleman of Essex, named Henry Winstanley, came forward, and, having obtained the necessary legal powers, began the great work of building on the wave-lashed rock.

Winstanley was an eccentric as well as a bold man. He undoubtedly possessed an ingenious mechanical mind, which displayed itself very much in practical joking. It is said of him that he made a machine, the spring of which was attached to an old slipper, which lay (apparently by chance) on the floor of his bedroom. If a visitor kicked this out of his way, a phantom instantly arose from the floor! He also constructed a chair which seized every one who sat down in it with its arms, and held them fast; and in his garden he had an arbour which went afloat in a neighbouring canal when any one entered it! As might have been expected, Winstanley's lighthouse was a curious affair, not well adapted to withstand the fury of the waves. It was highly ornamented, and resembled a Chinese pagoda much more than a lighthouse. Nevertheless it must be said to the credit of this bold man, that after facing and overcoming, during six years, difficulties and dangers which up to that time had not been heard of, he finished his lighthouse, proved hereby the possibility of that which had been previously deemed impossible, and gave to mankind a noble example of enterprise, daring, and perseverance.

Our friend John Potter had, from the commencement, rendered able assistance in the dangerous work as a stone cutter, and he could not help feeling as if he had been deserted by an old friend that night when the boat went off to the rock without him.

It was in November 1703, when Winstanley expressed the wish that he might experience, in his lighthouse, the greatest storm that ever blew. On the 26th of that month his wish was granted! That night there arose one of the fiercest gales that ever strewed our shores with wrecks and corpses. The day before the storm, there were indications of its approach, so John Potter went down to the shore to look with some anxiety at the lighthouse. There it stood, as the sun went down, like a star on the horizon, glimmering above the waste of foaming water. When the dark pall and the driving sprays of that terrible night hid it from view, John turned his back on the sea and sought the shelter of his humble home.

It was a cheery home though a poor one, for Mrs Potter was a good housewife, despite her sharp temper; and the threatening aspect of the weather had subdued her somewhat.

"You wouldn't like to be a lighthouse-keeper on a night like this, John, would you?" asked Mrs Potter, as she busied herself with supper.

"May be not: but I would be content to take things as they are sent. Anyhow, I mean to apply for the situation, because I like the notion of the quiet life, and the wage will be good as well as sure, which will be a matter of comfort to you, old girl. You often complain, you know, of the uncertainty of my present employment."

"Ay, but I'd rather 'ave that uncertainty than see you run the risk of bein' drownded in a light'ouse," said Mrs Potter, glancing uneasily at the window, which rattled violently as the fury of the gale increased.

"Oh, faither," exclaimed Tommy, pausing with a potato halfway to his mouth, as he listened partly in delight and partly in dread to the turmoil without: "I wish I was a man that I might go with 'ee to live in the light'ouse. Wot fun it would be to hear the gale roarin' out *there*, an' to see the big waves *so close*, an' to feel the house shake, and—oh!"

The last syllable expressed partly his inability to say more, and partly his horror at seeing the fire blown almost into the room!

For some time past the smoke had poured down the chimney, but the last burst convinced John Potter that it was high time to extinguish the fire altogether.

This accomplished, he took down an old family Bible from a shelf, and had worship, for he was a man who feared and loved God. Earnestly did he pray, for he had a son in the coasting trade whom he knew to be out upon the raging sea that night, and he did not forget his friends upon the Eddystone Rock.

"Get thee to bed, lass," he said when he had concluded. "I'll sit up an' read the word. My eyes could not close this night."

Poor Mrs Potter meekly obeyed. How strangely the weather had changed her! Even her enemies—and she had many—would have said there was some good in her after all, if they had seen her with a tear trickling down her ruddy cheek as she thought of her sailor boy.

Day broke at last. The gale still raged with an excess of fury that was absolutely appalling. John Potter wrapped himself in a tarpaulin coat and sou'wester preparatory to going out.

"I'll go with 'ee, John," said his wife, touching him on the shoulder.

"You couldn't face it, Martha," said John. "I thowt ye had bin asleep."

"No: I've bin thinkin' of our dear boy. I can face it well enough."

"Come, then: but wrap well up. Let Tommy come too: I see he's gettin' ready."

Presently the three went out. The door almost burst off its hinges when it was opened, and it required John's utmost strength to reclose it.

Numbers of people, chiefly men, were already hurrying to the beach. Clouds of foam and salt spray were whirled madly in the air, and, carried far inland, and slates and cans were dashing on the pavements. Men tried to say to each other that they had never seen such a storm, but the gale caught their voices; away, and seemed to mingle them all up in one prolonged roar. On gaining the beach they could see nothing at first but the heavings of the maddened sea, whose billows mingled their thunders with the wind. Sand, gravel, and spray almost blinded them, but as daylight increased they caught glimpses of the foam above the rock.

"God help us!" said John, solemnly, as he and his wife and child sought shelter under the lee of a wall: "*the light'ouse is gone!*"

It was too true. The Eddystone lighthouse had been swept completely away, with the unfortunate Winstanley and all his men: not a vestige, save a fragment of chain-cable, remained on the fatal rock to tell that such a building had ever been.

Chapter Two.

Beginning of Rudyerd's Lighthouse.

The terrible gale which swept away the first lighthouse that was built on the Eddystone Rock, gave ample proof of the evils resulting from the want of such a building. Just after the structure fell, a vessel, named the "Winchelsea," homeward bound, approached the dreaded rock. Trusting, doubtless, to the light which had been destroyed so recently, she held on her course, struck, split in two, and went down with every soul on board.

The necessity for building another tower was thus made; as it were, urgently obvious; nevertheless, nearly four years elapsed before any one was found with sufficient courage and capacity to attempt the dangerous and difficult enterprise.

During this period, our friend John Potter, being a steady, able man, found plenty of work at the docks of Plymouth; but he often cast a wistful glance in the direction of "the Rock" and sighed to think of the tower that had perished, and the numerous wrecks that had occurred in consequence; for, not only had some vessels struck on the Rock itself, but others, keeping too far off its dreaded locality, were wrecked on the coast of France. John Potter's sigh, it must be confessed, was also prompted, in part, by the thought that his dreams of a retired and peaceful life as a light-keeper were now destined never to be realised.

Returning home one evening, somewhat wearied, he flung his huge frame into a stout arm chair by the fireside, and exclaimed, "Heigho!"

"Deary me, John, what ails you to-night?" asked the faithful Martha, who was, as of yore, busy with the supper.

"Nothin' partikler, Martha; only I've had a hard day of it, an I'm glad to sit down. Was Isaac Dorkin here to-day?"

"No, 'e wasn't. I wonder you keep company with that man," replied Mrs Potter, testily; "he's for ever quarrelling with 'ee, John."

"No doubt he is, Martha; but we always make it up again; an' it don't do for a man to give up his comrades just because they have sharp words now and then. Why, old girl, you and I are always havin' a spurt o' that sort off and on; yet I don't ever talk of leavin' ye on that account."

To this Martha replied, "Fiddlesticks;" and said that she didn't believe in the friendship of people who were always fighting and making it up again; that for her part she would rather have no friends at all, she wouldn't; and that she had a settled conviction, she had, that Isaac Dorkin would come to a bad end at last.

"I hope not, Martha; but in the meantime he has bin the means of gettin' me some work to do that is quite to my liking."

"What may that be, John?" asked Mrs Potter in surprise.

"I'll tell you when we're at supper," said John with a smile; for he knew from experience that his better half was in a fitter state to swallow unpleasant news when engaged in swallowing her meals than at any other time.

"Where is Tommy?" he added, looking round at the quantity of chips which littered the floor.

"Where is 'e?" repeated Mrs Potter, in a tone of indignation. "Where would you expect 'im to be but after mischief? 'E's at the mod'l, of course; always at it; never at hanythingk else a'most."

"No!" exclaimed John, in affected surprise. "Wasn't he at school to-day?"

"O yes, of course 'e was at school."

"An' did he git his lessons for to-morrow after comin' 'ome?"

"I suppose 'e did."

"Ah then, he does something else *sometimes*, eh?"

Mrs Potter's reply was interrupted by Tommy himself emerging from a closet, which formed his workshop and in which he was at that time busy with a model of Winstanley's lighthouse, executed from the drawings and descriptions by his father, improved by his own brilliant fancy.

Four years make a marked difference on a boy in the early stage of life. He was now nearly ten, and well grown, both intellectually and physically, for his age.

"Well, Tommy, how d'ee git on wi' the light-'ouse?" asked his father.

"Pretty well, faither: but it seems to me that Mr Winstanley had too many stickin'-out poles, an' curlywurleys, an' things o' that sort about it."

"Listen to that now," said Mrs Potter, with a look of contempt, as they all sat down to supper: "what ever does the boy mean by curlywurleys?"

"You've seed Isaac Dorkin's nose, mother?"

"Of course I 'ave: what then?"

"Well, it goes in at the top and out at the middle and curls up at the end: that's curlywurley," said Tommy, with a grin, as he helped himself to a large potato.

"The boy is right, Martha," said John, laughing, "for a lighthouse should be as round an' as smooth as a ship's bow, with nothin' for wind or water to lay hold on. But now I'll tell 'ee of this noo situation."

Both mother and son looked inquiringly up, but did not speak, being too busy and hungry.

"Well, this is how it came about. I met Isaac Dorkin on my way to the docks this mornin', an' he says to me, says he, 'John, I met a gentleman who is makin' very partikler inquiries about the Eddystone Rock: his name he says is Rudyerd, and he wants to hire a lot o' first-rate men to begin a new—'"

"A noo light'ouse!" exclaimed Mrs Potter, with sudden energy, bringing her fist down on the table with such force that the dishes rattled again. "I know'd it: I did. I've 'ad a settled conviction that if ever they begun to put up another 'ouse on that there rock, you would 'ave your finger in it! And now it'll be the old story over again: out in all weathers, gettin' yer limbs bruised, if yer neck ain't broke; comin' 'ome like a drownded rat, no regular hours or meals! Oh John, John!"

Mrs Potter stopped at this point to recover breath and make up her mind whether to storm or weep. Heaving a deep sigh she did neither, but went on with her supper in sad silence.

"Don't take on like that, duckey," said John, stretching his long arm across the table and patting his wife's shoulder. "It won't be so bad as that comes to, and it will bring steady work, besides lots o' money."

"Go on with the story, faither," said Tommy, through a potato, while his eyes glittered with excitement.

"It ain't a story, lad. However, to make it short I may come to the pint at once. Isaac got engaged himself and mentioned my name to Mr Rudyerd, who took the trouble to ferret me out in the docks and—and in fact engaged me for the work, which is to begin next week."

"Capital!" exclaimed Tommy. "Oh, how I wish I was old enough to go too!"

"Time enough, lad: every dog shall have his day, as the proverb says."

Mrs Potter said nothing, but sighed, and sought comfort in another cup of tea.

Meanwhile John continued his talk in an easy, off hand sort of way, between bite.

"This Mr Rudyerd, you must know (pass the loaf, Tommy: thank 'ee), is a Cornish man—and fine, straightforward, go-ahead fellows them Cornish men are, though I'm not one myself. Ah, you needn't turn up your pretty nose, Mrs Potter; I would rather have bin born in Cornwall than any other county in England, if I'd had my choice. Howsever, that ain't possible now. Well, it seems that Mr Rudyerd is a remarkable sort of man. He came of poor an' dishonest parents, from whom he runned away in his young days, an' got employed by a Plymouth gentleman, who became a true father to him, and got him a good edication in readin', writin', an' mathematics. Ah, Tommy, my son, many a time have I had cause for to regret that nobody gave me a good edication!"

"Fiddlesticks!" exclaimed Mrs Potter, rousing up at this. "You've got edication enough for your station in life, and a deal more than most men in the same trade. You oughtn't for to undervally yourself, John. I'd back you against all your acquaintance in the matter of edication, I would, so don't talk any more nonsense like that."

Mrs Potter concluded by emphatically stabbing a potato with her fork, and beginning to peel it.

John smiled sadly and shook his head, but he was too wise a man to oppose his wife on such a point.

"However, Tommy," he continued, "I'll not let *you* have the same regrets in after life, my son: God helping me, you shall have a good; edication. Well, as I was sayin', John Rudyerd the runaway boy became Mister Rudyerd the silk-mercer on Ludgate Hill, London, and now he's goin' to build a noo light'ouse on the Eddystun."

"He'd do better to mind his shop," said Mrs Potter.

"He must be a strange man," observed Tommy, "to be both a silk-mercer and an engineer."

Tommy was right: Mr Rudyerd was indeed a strange man, for the lighthouse which he ultimately erected on the Eddystone Rock proved that, although not a professional engineer, and although he never attempted any other great work of the kind, he nevertheless possessed engineering talent of the highest order: a fact which must of course have been known to Captain Lovet, the gentleman who selected him for the arduous undertaking.

The corporation of the Trinity House, who managed the lighthouses on the English coast, had let the right to build on the Eddystone, for a period of 99 years, to this Captain Lovet, who appointed Mr Rudyerd to do the work.

It was a clear calm morning in July 1706 when the boat put off for the first time to "the Rock," with the men and materials for commencing the lighthouse. Our friend John Potter sat at the helm. Opposite to him sat his testy friend, Isaac Dorkin, pulling the stroke oar. Mr Rudyerd and his two assistant engineers sat on either hand, conversing on the subject that filled the thoughts of all. It was a long hard pull, even on a calm day, but stout oars and strong arms soon carried them out to the rock. Being low water at the time, a good deal of it was visible, besides several jagged peaks of the black forbidding ridge of which the Eddystone forms a part.

But calm though it was, the party could plainly see that the work before them would be both difficult and dangerous. A slight swell from the open sea caused a long smooth glassy wave to roll solemnly forward every minute or two, and launch itself in thunder on the weather side, sending its spray right over the rock at times, so that a landing on that side would have been impossible. On the lee side, however, the boat found a sort of temporary harbour. Here they landed, but not altogether without mishap. Isaac Dorkin, who had made himself conspicuous, during the row out, for caustic remarks, and a tendency to contradict, slipped his foot on a piece of seaweed and fell into the water, to the great glee of most of his comrades.

"Ah, then, sarves you right," cried Teddy Maroon, a little Irishman, one of the joiners.

The others laughed, and so did John Potter; but he also stretched out a helping hand and pulled Dorkin out of the sea.

This little incident tended to increase the spirits of the party as they commenced preliminary operations.

The form of the little mass of rock on which they had to build was very unfavourable. Not only was it small—so small that the largest circle which it was possible to draw on it was only twenty-five feet six inches in diameter, but its surface sloped so much as to afford a very insecure foundation for any sort of building, even if the situation had been an unexposed one.

The former builder, Winstanley, had overcome this difficulty by fastening a circle of strong iron posts into the solid rock, but the weight of his building, coupled with the force of the sea, had snapped these, and thus left the structure literally to slide off its foundation. The ends of these iron posts, and a bit of chain firmly imbedded in a cleft of the rock, were all that the new party of builders found remaining of the old lighthouse. Rudyerd determined to guard against a similar catastrophe, by cutting the rock into a succession of flat steps or terraces, so that the weight of his structure should rest perpendicularly on its foundation.

Stormy weather interrupted and delayed him, but he returned with his men again and again to the work, and succeeded in advancing it very considerably during the first year—that is to say, during the few weeks of the summer of that year, in which winds and waves permitted the work to go on.

Many adventures, both ludicrous and thrilling, had these enterprising men while they toiled, by snatches as it were, sometimes almost under water, and always under difficulties; but we are constrained to pass these by, in silence, in order to devote our space to the more important and stirring incidents in the history of this the second lighthouse on the Eddystone,—one of which incidents bade fair to check the progress of the building for an indefinite period of time, and well-nigh brought the career of our hero, John Potter, and his mates to an abrupt close.

Chapter Three.

A Violent Interruption.

The incident referred to in our last chapter occurred on the afternoon of a calm summer day. Early that morning, shortly after daybreak, Mr Rudyerd, with his engineers and workmen, put off in the boat to resume operations on the rock after a lapse of nearly a week, during which period rough weather had stopped the work. They landed without difficulty, the calm being so complete that there was only a little sea caused by the heavy swell on the south-west side of the Eddystone Rock, the leeside being as quiet as a pond.

"It's not often we have weather like this sir," observed John Potter to Mr Rudyerd, as the heavily-laden boat approached the landing place.

"True, John; a few weeks like this would enable us almost to complete the courses," replied the engineer. "Easy, lads, easy! If you run her up so fast you'll stave in the planks. Stand by with the fender, Teddy!"

"Ay, ay, sir!" cried the man, springing up and seizing a stuffed canvas ball, which he swung over the gunwale just in time to prevent the boat's side from grazing the rock. "There now: jump out wi' the painter; man alive!" said Teddy, addressing himself to Isaac Dorkin, who was naturally slow in his movements, "you'll go souse between the boat an' the rock av ye don't be smarter nor that."

Dorkin made some grumbling reply as he stepped upon the rock, and fastened the painter to a ring-bolt. His comrades sprang after him, and while some began to heave the tools from the boat, others busied themselves round the base of the column, which had by that time risen to a considerable height. It looked massive enough to bid defiance to wind and waves, however fierce their fury. Some such thought must have passed through Mr Rudyerd's mind just then, for a satisfied smile lighted up his usually grave features as he directed the men to arrange the tackle of the crane, by which the stones were to be removed from the boat to their place on the building. They were all quickly at work; for they knew from experience how suddenly their operations might be cut short by a gale.

In order that the reader may fully understand the details of the event which occurred that afternoon, it is necessary that he should know the nature of the structure, and the height to which, at that time, it had proceeded; and while we are on the subject, we may as well state a few facts connected with the foundation and superstructure, which cannot fail to interest all who take pleasure in contemplating man's efforts to overcome almost insuperable difficulties.

As we have said, the sloping foundation of the building was cut into a series of terraces or steps. There were seven of these. The first operation was the cutting of thirty-six holes in the solid rock, into which iron hold-fasts were securely fixed. The cutting of these holes or sockets was ingeniously managed. First, three small holes were drilled into the rock; and then these were broken into one large hole, which was afterwards smoothed, enlarged, and *undercut*, so as to be of dovetail form; the size of each being 7 and a half inches broad and 2 and a half inches wide at the top, and an inch broader at the bottom. They were about sixteen inches deep. Thirty-six massive malleable iron hold-fasts were then inserted, and wedged into the places thus prepared for them, besides being filled up with lead, so that no force of any kind could draw them out. The next proceeding was to place beams of solid oak timber, lengthwise, on the first *step*, thus bringing it level with the second step. Timbers of the same kind were then placed above and across these, bringing the level up to the third step. The next "course" of timbers was again laid, lengthwise, bringing the level to the fourth step, and so on to the seventh, above which two completely circular timber courses were laid, thus making a perfectly flat and solid foundation on which the remainder of the column might rest. The building, therefore, had no tendency to slide, even although it had not been held in its place by the thirty-six hold-fasts before mentioned. In addition to this, the various courses of timber were fastened to the rock and to each other by means of numerous iron cramps and bolts, and wooden trenails.

It was well known to Mr Rudyerd, however, that it was not possible to fit his timbers so perfectly to the rock and to each other as to exclude water altogether; and that if the water should manage to find entrance, it would exert a tremendous lifting power, which, coupled with the weight of the falling billows, would be apt to sweep his foundation away. He resolved, therefore, to counteract this by means of *weight*; and, in order to do this, he next piled five courses of Cornish moor-stone above the timber courses. The stones were huge blocks, which, when laid and fastened in one solid stratum, weighed 120 tons. They were not laid in cement; but each block was fastened to its fellow by joints and similar to the first. The whole of this fabric was built round a strong central mast or pole, which rose from the rock. The two timber courses above described terminated the "solid" part of the lighthouse. It rose to the height of about fourteen feet from the rock, at the centre of the building.

At this point in the structure; namely, at the top of the "solid," the door was begun on the east side; and a central "well-hole" was left, where the stair leading to the rooms above was ultimately built. The door itself was reached by a strong iron stair of open work, outside, through which the sea could easily wash.

After the solid was completed, other five courses of moor-stone were laid, which weighed about eighty-six tons. It was in these that the door-way and well-hole were made. Two more courses of wood followed, covering the door-head; and on these, four more courses of stone, weighing sixty-seven tons; then several courses of timber, with a floor of oak plank, three inches thick, over all, forming the floor of the first apartment, which was the store-room. This first floor was thirty-three feet above the rock.

The upper part of the column, containing its four rooms, was by no means so strong as the lower part, being composed chiefly of the timber uprights in which the building was encased from top to bottom. These uprights, numbering seventy-one, were massive beams; about a foot broad and nine inches thick at the bottom, and diminishing towards the top. Their seams were caulked like those of a ship, and they gave to the lighthouse when finished the appearance of an elegant fluted column. The top of the column, on which rested the lantern, rose, when finished, to about sixty-three feet above the highest part of the rock.

We have thought proper to give these details in this place, but at the time of which we write, none of the outside timbers had been set up, and the edifice had only reached that point immediately above the "solid," where the doorway and the "well-hole" began. Here a large crane had been fixed, and two of the men were up there working the windlass, by which the heavy blocks of moor-stone were raised to their places.

The signal had been given to hoist one of these, when Isaac Dorkin, who stood beside the stone, suddenly uttered a loud cry, and shouted, "hold on! Ease off up there! Hold o-o-on! D'ye hear?"

"Arrah! howld yer noise, an' I'll hear better," cried Teddy Maroon, looking over the top edge of the lighthouse.

"My thumb's caught i' the chain!" yelled Dorkin. "Ease it off."

"Och! poor thing," exclaimed Teddy, springing back and casting loose the chain. "Are ye aisy now?" he cried, again looking down at his friend.

"All right: hoist away!" shouted Stobbs, another of the men, who could scarce refrain from laughing at the rueful countenance of his comrade as he surveyed his crushed thumb.

Up went the stone, and while it was ascending some of the men brought forward another to follow it.

"There comes the boat," observed Mr Rudyerd to one of his assistant engineers, as he shut up a pocket telescope with which he had been surveying the distant shore. "I find it necessary to leave you to-day, Mr Franks, rather earlier than usual; but that matters little, as things are going smoothly here. See that you keep the men at work as long as possible. If the swell that is beginning to rise should increase, it may compel you to knock off before dark, but I hope it won't."

"It would be well, sir, I think," said Franks, "to make John Potter overseer in place of Williamson; he is a better and steadier man. If you have no objection—"

"None in the least," replied Rudyerd. "I have thought of promoting Potter for some time past. Make the change by all means."

"Please, sir," said Williamson, approaching at that moment, "I've just been at the top of the building an' observed a French schooner bearing down from the south-west."

"Well, what of that?" demanded Rudyerd.

"Why, sir," said Williamson with some hesitation in his manner, "p'raps it's a man-of-war, sir."

"And if it be so, what then?" said Rudyerd with a smile; "you don't suppose they'll fire a broadside at an unfinished lighthouse, do you? or are you afraid they'll take the Eddystone Rock in tow, and carry you into a French port?"

"I don't know, sir," replied Williamson with an offended look; "I only thought that as we are at war with France just now, it was my duty to report what I had seen."

"Quite right, quite right," replied Rudyerd, good-humouredly, "I'll record the fact in our journal. Meanwhile see that the men don't have their attention taken up with it."

By this time the small boat, which the chief engineer had ordered to come off to take him on shore, was alongside the rock. The swell had risen so much that although there was not a breath of wind, the surf was beating violently on the south-west side, and even in the sheltered nook, which was styled by courtesy the harbour, there was sufficient commotion to render care in fending off with the boat-hook necessary. Meanwhile the men wrought like tigers, taking no note of their chief's departure—all, except Williamson, being either ignorant of, or indifferent to, the gradual approach of the French schooner, which drifted slowly towards them with the tide.

Thus work and time went on quietly. Towards the afternoon, Teddy Maroon wiped the perspiration from his heated brow and looked abroad upon the sea, while the large hook of his crane was descending for another stone. An expression of intense earnestness wrinkled his visage as he turned suddenly to Stobbs, his companion at the windlass, and exclaimed:—

"Sure that's a Frenchman over there."

"That's wot it is, Ted, an' no mistake," said Stobbs. "I had a'most forgot about the war and the Mounseers."

"Ah then, it's not goin' to attack us ye are, is it? Never!" exclaimed Teddy in surprise, observing that two boats had been lowered from the schooner's davits into which men were crowding.

The question was answered in a way that could not be misunderstood. A puff of white smoke burst from the vessel's side, and a cannon shot went skipping over the sea close past the lighthouse, at the same time the French flag was run up and the two boats, pushing off, made straight for the rock.

Teddy and his comrade ran down to the foot of the building, where the other men were arming themselves hastily with crowbars and large chips of stone. Marshalling the men together, the assistant engineer, who was a fiery little fellow, explained to them how they ought to act.

"My lads," said he, "the surf has become so strong, by good luck, that it is likely to capsize the enemy's boats before they get here. In which case they'll be comfortably drowned, and we can resume our work; but if they manage to reach the rock, we'll retire behind the lighthouse to keep clear of their musket balls; and, when they attempt to land, rush at 'em, and heave 'em all into the sea. It's like enough that they're more numerous than we, but you all know that one Englishman is a match for three Frenchmen any day."

A general laugh and cheer greeted this address, and then they all took shelter behind the lighthouse. Meanwhile, the two boats drew near. The lightest one was well in advance. On it came, careering on the crest of a large glassy wave. Now was the time for broaching-to and upsetting, but the boat was cleverly handled. It was launched into the "harbour" on a sea of foam.

Most of the Englishmen, on seeing this, ran to oppose the landing.

"Surrender!" shouted an officer with a large moustache, standing up in the bow of the boat.

"Never!" replied Mr Franks, defiantly.

"Hooray!" yelled Teddy Maroon, flourishing his crowbar.

At this the officer gave an order: the Frenchmen raised their muskets, and the Englishmen scampered back to their place of shelter, laughing like school-boys engaged in wild play. Teddy Maroon, whose fertile brain was always devising some novelty or other, ran up to his old post at the windlass, intending to cast a large mass of stone into the boat when it neared the rock, hoping thereby to knock a hole through its bottom; but before he reached his perch, a breaker burst into the harbour and overturned the boat, leaving her crew to struggle towards the rock. Some of them were quickly upon it, grappling with the Englishmen who rushed forward to oppose the landing. Seeing this, Teddy hurled his mass of stone at the head of an unfortunate Frenchman, whom he narrowly missed, and then, uttering a howl, ran down to join in the fray. The French commander, a powerful man, was met knee-deep in the water, by Isaac Dorkin, whom he struck down with the hilt of his sword, and poor Isaac's grumbling career would certainly have come to an end then and there, had not John Potter, who had already hurled two Frenchmen back into the sea, run to the rescue, and, catching his friend by the hair of the head, dragged him on the rock. At that moment Teddy Maroon dashed at the French officer, caught his uplifted sword-arm by the wrist, and pushed him back into the sea just as he was in the act of making a savage cut at John Potter. Before the latter had dragged his mate quite out of danger he was grappled with by another Frenchman, and they fell struggling to the ground, while a third came up behind Teddy with a boat-hook, and almost took him by surprise; but Teddy turned in time, caught the boat-hook in his left hand, and, flattening the Frenchman's nose with his right, tumbled him over and ran to assist in repelling another party of the invaders who were making good their landing at the other side of the rock.

Thus the "skrimmage," as John Potter styled it, became general. Although out-numbered, the Englishmen were getting the best of it, when the second boat plunged into the so-called harbour, and in a few seconds the rock was covered with armed men. Of course the Englishmen were overpowered. Their tools were collected and put into the boat. With some difficulty the first boat was righted. The Englishmen were put into it, with a strong guard of marines, and then the whole party were carried on board the French schooner, which turned out to be a privateer.

Thus were the builders of the Eddystone lighthouse carried off as prisoners of war to France, and their feelings may be gathered from the last remark of Teddy Maroon, who, as the white cliffs of England were fading from his view, exclaimed bitterly, "Och hone! I'll never see owld Ireland no more!"

Note. It may be as well to state, at this point, that the incidents here related, and indeed all the important incidents of our tale, are founded on, we believe, well authenticated facts.

Chapter Four.

Unlooked-for Deliverance.

Behold, then, our lighthouse-builders entering a French port; Teddy Maroon looking over the side of the vessel at the pier to which they are drawing near, and grumbling sternly at his sad fate; John Potter beside him, with his arms crossed, his eyes cast down, and his thoughts far away with the opinionated Martha and the ingenious Tommy; Mr Franks and the others standing near; all dismal and silent.

"You not seem for like ver moche to see la belle France," said the French officer with the huge moustache, addressing Teddy.

"It's little Teddy Maroon cares whether he sees Bell France or Betsy France," replied the Irishman, impudently. "No thanks *to you* aither for givin' me the chance. Sure it's the likes o' you that bring war into disgrace intirely; goin' about the say on yer own hook, plunderin' right an' left. It's pirate, and not privateers, ye should be called, an' it's myself that would string ye all at the yard-arm av I only had me own way."

"Hah!" exclaimed the Frenchman, with a scowl: "but by goot fortune you not have your own vay. Perhaps you change you mind ven you see de inside of French prisons, ha!"

"Perhaps I won't; ha!" cried Teddy, mimicking his captor. "Go away wid yez, an' attind to yer own business."

The Frenchman turned angrily away. In a few seconds more they were alongside the pier, and a gangway was run on board.

The first man who stepped on this gangway was a tall powerful gendarme, with a huge cocked hat, and a long cavalry sabre, the steel scabbard of which clattered magnificently as he stalked along. Now it chanced that this dignified official slipped his foot on the gangway, and, to the horror of all observers, fell into the water.

Impulsiveness was a part of Teddy Maroon's enthusiastic nature. He happened to be gazing in admiration at the gendarme when he fell. In another moment he had plunged overboard after him, caught him by the collar, and held him up.

The gendarme could not swim. In the first agony of fear he threw about his huge limbs, and almost drowned his rescuer.

"Be aisy, won't 'ee!" shouted Ted, holding him at arm's length, and striving to keep out of his grasp. At the same time he dealt him a hearty cuff on the ear.

The words and the action appeared to have a sedative effect on the gendarme, who at once became passive, and in a few minutes the rescuer and the rescued stood dripping on the schooner's deck.

"Thank 'ee, my friend," said the gendarme in English, extending his hand.

"Och, ye're an Irishman!" exclaimed Teddy eagerly, as he grasped the offered hand. "But sure," he added, in an altered tone, dropping the hand and glancing at the man's uniform, "ye must be a poor-spirited craitur to forsake yer native land an' become a mounseer."

"Ireland is not my native land, and I am not an Irishman," said the gendarme, with a smile. "My mother was Irish, but my father was French, and I was born in Paris. It is true that I spent many years in Ireland among my mother's relations, so that I speak your language, but I am more French than Irish."

"Humph! more's the pity," said Teddy. "If there was but wan drop o' me blood Irish an' all the rest o' me French, I'd claim to be an Irishman. If I'd known what ye was I'd have let ye sink, I would. Go along: I don't think much of yez."

"Perhaps not," replied the gendarme, twirling his long moustache with a good-humoured smile; "nevertheless I think a good deal of you, my fine fellow. Farewell, I shall see you again."

"Ye needn't trouble yerself," replied Teddy, flinging off, testily.

It was quite evident that the unfortunate Irishman found it hard to get reconciled to his fate. He could scarcely be civil to his mates in misfortune, and felt a strong disposition to wrench the sword from his captor's hand, cut off his moustached head, and then, in the language of desperate heroes of romance, "sell his life dearly." He refrained, however, and was soon after marched along with his mates to the stronghold of the port, at the door of which the French commander handed them over to the jailor, wishing Teddy all health and happiness, with a broad grin, as he bid him farewell.

Our unfortunates crossed a stone court with walls that appeared to rise into the clouds; then they traversed a dark stone passage, at the end of which stood an open door with a small stone cell beyond. Into this they were desired to walk, and as several bayonet points glittered in the passage behind them, they felt constrained to obey. Then locks were turned, and bars were drawn, and bolts were shot. The heavy heels of the jailer and guard were heard retiring. More locks and bars and bolts were turned and drawn and shot at the farther end of the stone passage, after which all remained still as the grave.

"Och hone!" groaned Teddy, looking round at his companions, as he sat on a stone seat, the picture of despair: "To be kilt is a trifle; to fight is a pleasure; to be hanged is only a little trying to the narves. But to be shut up in a stone box in a furrin land—"

Words failed him here, but another groan told eloquently of the bitterness of the spirit within.

"We must just try to be as cheery as we can, mates," said John Potter. "The Lord can deliver us out o' worse trouble than this if He sees fit."

"Oh, it's all very well for you to talk like that," growled Isaac Dorkin, "but I don't believe the Almighty is goin' to pull down stone walls and iron gates to set us free, an' you know that we haven't a friend in all France to help us."

"I *don't* know that, Isaac. It certainly seems very unlikely that any one should start up to befriend us here, but with God all things are possible. At the worst, I know that if we are to remain here, it's His will that we should."

"Humph! I wish ye much comfort o' the thought: it doesn't give much to me," remarked Stobbs.

Here, Mr Franks, who had hitherto sat in sad silence, brightened up, and said, "Well, well, lads, don't let us make things worse by disputing. Surely each man is entitled to draw comfort from any source he chooses. For my part, I agree with John Potter, in this at all events,—that we should try to be as cheery as we can, and make the best of it."

"Hear, hear!" exclaimed the others. Acting on this advice, they soon began to feel a little less miserable. They had straw to sleep on, and were allowed very poor fare; but there was a sufficiency of it. The first night passed, and the second day; after which another fit of despair seized some of the party. Then John Potter managed to cheer them up a bit, and as he never went about without a small Testament in his pocket, he was able to lighten the time by reading portions of it aloud. After that they took to relating their "lives and adventures" to each other, and then the inventive spirits among them took to "spinning long-winded yarns." Thus a couple of weeks passed away, during which these unfortunate prisoners of war went through every stage of feeling between hope and despair over and over again.

During one of his despairing moods, Teddy Maroon declared that he had now given up all hope, and that the first chance he got, he would kill himself, for he was quite certain that nobody would ever be able to find out where they were, much less "get them out of that fig."

But Teddy was wrong, as the sequel will show.

Let us leap now, good reader, to the Tuileries,—into the apartments of Louis XIV. From a prison to a palace is an unusual leap, no doubt, though the reverse is by no means uncommon! The old King is pacing his chamber in earnest thought, addressing an occasional remark to his private Secretary. The subject that occupies him is the war, and the name of England is frequently on his lips. The Secretary begs leave to bring a particular letter under the notice of the King. The Secretary speaks in French, of course, but there is a peculiarly rich tone and emphasis in his voice which a son of the Green Isle would unhesitatingly pronounce to be "the brogue."

"Read it," says the King hurriedly: "but first tell me, who writes?"

"A gendarme, sire: a poor relation of mine."

"Ha: an Irishman?"

"No, sire: but his mother was Irish."

"Well, read," says the King.

The Secretary reads: "Dear Terrence, will you do me the favour to bring a matter before the King? The commander of a French privateer has done an act worthy of a buccaneer: he has attacked the men who were re-building the famous Eddystone lighthouse, and carried them prisoners of war into this port. I would not trouble you or the King about this, did I not know his Majesty too well to believe him capable of countenancing such a deed."

"What!" exclaims the King, turning abruptly, with a flush of anger on his countenance, "the Eddystone lighthouse, which so stands as to be of equal service to all nations having occasion to navigate the channel?"

"The same, sire; and the officer who has done this expects to be rewarded."

"Ha: he shall not be disappointed; he shall have his reward," exclaims the King. "Let him be placed in the prison where the English men now lie, to remain there during our pleasure; and set the builders of the Eddystone free. Let them have gifts, and all honourable treatment, to repay them for their temporary distress, and send them home, without delay, in the same vessel which brought them hither. We are indeed at war with England, but not with mankind!"

The commands of kings are, as a rule, promptly obeyed. Even although there were neither railways nor telegraphs in those days, many hours had not elapsed before the tall gendarme stood in the prison-cell where John Potter and his friends were confined. There was a peculiar twinkle in his eye, as he ordered a band of soldiers to act as a guard of honour in conducting the Englishmen to the best hotel in the town, where a sumptuous collation awaited them. Arrived there, the circumstances of their case were explained to them by the chief magistrate, who was in waiting to receive them and present them with certain gifts, by order of Louis XIV.

The fortunate men looked on at all that was done, ate their feast, and received their gifts in speechless amazement, until at length the gendarme (who acted as interpreter, and seemed to experience intense enjoyment at the whole affair) asked if they were ready to embark for England? To which Teddy Maroon replied, by turning to John Potter and saying, "I say, John, just give me a dig in the ribs, will 'ee: a good sharp one. It's of no use at all goin' on draimin' like this. It'll only make it the worse the longer I am o' wakin' up."

John Potter smiled and shook his head; but when he and his friends were conducted by their guard of honour on board of the schooner which had brought them there, and when they saw the moustached commander brought out of his cabin and led ashore in irons, and heard the click of the capstan as the vessel was warped out of harbour, and beheld the tall gendarme take off his cocked hat and wish them "*bon voyage*" as they passed the head of the pier, they at length became convinced that "it was all true;" and Teddy declared with enthusiastic emphasis, that "the mounseers were not such bad fellows after all!"

"Oh, John, John!" exclaimed Mrs Potter, about thirty hours after that, as she stood gazing in wild delight at a magnificent cashmere shawl which hung on her husband's arm, while Tommy was lost in admiration at the sight of a splendid inlaid ivory work-box, "where ever got 'ee such a helegant shawl?"

"From King Louis, of France, lass," said John, with a peculiar smile.

"Never!" said Mrs Potter, emphatically; and then she gave it forth as one of her settled convictions, that, "Kings wasn't such fools as to go makin' presents like that to poor working men."

However, John Potter, who had only just then presented himself before the eyes of his astonished spouse, stoutly asserted that it was true; and said that if she would set about getting something to eat, for he was uncommonly hungry, and if Tommy would leave off opening his mouth and eyes to such an unnecessary extent, he would tell them all about it. So Mrs Potter was convinced, and, for once, had her "settled convictions" unsettled; and the men returned to their work on the Eddystone; and a man-of-war was sent to cruise in the neighbourhood to guard them from misfortune in the future; and, finally, the Rudyerd lighthouse was completed.

Its total height, from the lowest side to the top of the ball on the lantern, was ninety-two feet, and its greatest diameter twenty-three feet four inches. It took about three years to build, having been commenced in 1706, the first light was put up in 1708, and the whole was completed in 1709.

Teddy Maroon was one of the first keepers, but he soon left to take charge of a lighthouse on the Irish coast. Thereupon John Potter made application for the post. He was successful over many competitors, and at last obtained the darling wish of his heart: he became principal keeper; his surly comrade, Isaac Dorkin, strange to say, obtaining the post of second keeper. Mrs Potter didn't like the change at first, as a matter of course.

"But you'll come to like it, Martha," John would say when they referred to the subject, "'Absence,' you know, 'makes the heart grow fonder.' We'll think all the more of each other when we meet during my spells ashore, at the end of every two months."

Tommy also objected very much at first, but he could not alter his father's intentions; so John Potter went off to the Eddystone rock, and for a long time took charge of the light that cast its friendly beams over the sea every night thereafter, through storm and calm, for upwards of six-and-forty years.

That John's life in the lighthouse was not all that he had hoped for will become apparent in the next chapter.

Chapter Five.

A Terrible Situation.

There were four rooms and a lantern in Rudyerd's lighthouse. The second room was that which was used most by John Potter and his mate Isaac Dorkin: it was the kitchen, dining room, and parlour, all in one. Immediately below it was the store-room, and just above it the dormitory.

The general tenor of the life suited John exactly: he was a quiet-spirited, meditative, religious man; and, although quite willing to face difficulties, dangers, and troubles like a man, when required to do so, he did not see it to be his duty to thrust himself unnecessarily into these circumstances. There were plenty of men, he was wont to say, who loved bustle and excitement, and there were plenty of situations of that sort for them to fill; for his part, he loved peace and quiet; the Eddystone lighthouse offered both, and why should he not take advantage of the opportunity, especially when, by so doing, he would secure a pretty good and regular income for his wife and family.

John gave vent to an opinion which contained deeper truths than, at that time, he thought of. God has given to men their varied powers and inclinations, in order that they may use these powers and follow these inclinations. Working rightly, man is a perfect machine: it is only "the fall" which has twisted all things awry. There is no sin in feeling an intense desire for violent physical action, or in gratifying that desire when we can do so in accordance with the revealed will of God; but there is sin in gratifying it in a wrong way; in committing burglary for instance, or in prize-fighting, or in helping others to fight in a cause with which we have no right to interfere. Again, it is not wrong to desire peace and quiet, and to wish for mental and spiritual and physical repose; but it is decidedly wrong to stand by with your hands in your pockets when an innocent or helpless one is being assaulted by ruffians; to sit quiet and do nothing when your neighbour's house is on fire; to shirk an unpleasant duty and leave some one else to do it; or to lie a-bed when you should be up and at work.

All our powers were given to be used: our inclinations were intended to impel us in *certain* directions, and God's will and glory were meant to be our guide and aim. So the Scripture teaches, we think, in the parable of the talents, and in the words, "*Whatsoever* thy hand findeth to do, do it with thy might;" and, "Whether, therefore, ye eat, or drink, or whatsoever ye do, do all to the glory of God."

Our great fault lies in not consulting God's plan of arrangement. How often do we find that, in adopting certain lines of action, men consult only the pecuniary or social advantage; ignoring powers, or want of powers, and violating inclinations; and this even among professing Christians; while, among the unbelieving, God's will and glory are not thought of at all. And yet we wonder that so many well-laid plans miscarry, that so many promising young men and women "come to grief!" Forgetting that "the right man (or woman) in the right place" is an essential element in thorough success.

But, to return to John Potter. His conscience was easy as to his duty in becoming a lightkeeper, and the lighthouse was all that he could wish, or had hoped for. There was no disturbance from without, for the thick walls and solid foundation defied winds or waves to trouble him; save only in the matter of smoke, which often had a strong tendency to traverse the chimney in the wrong direction, but that was not worth mentioning! John found, however, that *sin* in the person of his mate marred his peace and destroyed his equanimity.

Isaac Dorkin did not find the life so much to his taste as he had expected. He became more grumpy than ever, and quarrelled with his friend on the slightest provocation; insomuch that at last John found it to be his wisest plan to let him alone. Sometimes, in consequence of this pacific resolve, the two men would spend a whole month without uttering a word to each other; the one in the sulks, the other waiting until he should come out of them.

Their duties were light, but regular. During the day they found a sufficiency of quiet occupation in cooking their food, cleaning. The lighting apparatus—which consisted of a framework full of tallow candles,—and in keeping the building clean and orderly. At night they kept watch, each four hours at a time, while the other slept. While watching, John read his Bible and several books which had been given to him by Mr Rudyerd; or, in fine weather, paced round and round the gallery, just outside the lantern, in profound meditation. Dorkin also, during his watches, meditated much; he likewise grumbled a good deal, and smoked continuously. He was not a bad fellow at bottom, however, and sometimes he and Potter got on very amicably. At such seasons John tried to draw his mate into religious talk, but without success. Thus, from day to day and year to year, these two men stuck to their post, until eleven years had passed away.

One day, about the end of that period, John Potter, who, having attained to the age of fifty-two, was getting somewhat grey, though still in full strength and vigour, sat at his chimney corner beside his buxom and still blooming wife. His fireside was a better one than in days of yore,— thanks to Tommy, who had become a flourishing engineer: Mrs Potter's costume was likewise much better in condition and quality than it used to be; thanks, again, to Tommy, who was a grateful and loving son.

"Well, Martha, I've had a pleasant month ashore, lass: I wish that I hadn't to go off on relief to-morrow."

"Why not leave it altogether, then, John? You've no occasion to continue a light-keeper now that you've laid by so much, and Tommy is so well off and able to help us, an' willin' too—God bless him!"

"Amen to that, Martha. I have just bin thinkin' over the matter, and I've made up my mind that this is to be my last trip off to the Rock. I spoke to the superintendent last week, and it's all settled. Who d'ye think is to take my place?"

"I never could guess nothink, John: who?"

"Teddy Maroon: no less."

"What? an' 'im a' older man than yourself?"

"Ah, but it ain't the same Teddy. It's his eldest son, named after himself; an' so like what his father was when I last saw him, that I don't think I'd be able to tell which was which."

"Well, John, I'm glad to 'ear it; an' be sure that ye git 'ome, next relief before the thirty-first of October, for that's Tommy's wedding day, an' you know we fixed it a purpose to suit your time of being at 'ome. A sweet pair they'll make. Nora was born to be a lady: nobody would think but she is one, with 'er pretty winsome ways; and Tommy, who was twenty-five 'is very last birthday, is one of the 'andsomest men in Plymouth. I've a settled conviction, John, that he'll live to be a great man."

"You once had a settled conviction that he would come to a bad end," said Potter, with an arch smile.

"Go along with you, John!" retorted Mrs Potter.

"I'm just going," said John, rising and kissing his wife as he put on his hat; "and you may depend on it that I'll not miss dancing at our Tommy's wedding, if I can help it."

That night saw John Potter at his old post again—snuffing the candles on the Eddystone, and chatting with his old mate Dorkin beside the kitchen fire. One evening towards the end of October, John Potter and Isaac, having "lighted up," sat down to a game of draughts. It was blowing hard outside, and heavy breakers were bursting on the rock and sending thin spray as high as the lantern, but all was peace and comfort inside; even Isaac's grumpy spirit was calmer than usual.

"You seem dull to-night, mate," observed John, as they re-arranged the pieces for another game.

"I don't feel very well," said Dorkin, passing his hand over his brow languidly.

"You'd better turn in, then; an' I'll take half of your watch as well as my own."

"Thank 'ee kindly," said Dorkin in a subdued voice: "I'll take yer advice. Perhaps," he added slowly, "you'll read me a bit out o' *the Book*."

This was the first time that Isaac had expressed a desire to touch on religious subjects, or to hear the Bible read; and John, you may be sure, was only too glad to comply. After his mate had lain down, he read a small portion; but, observing that he seemed very restless, he closed the Bible and contented himself with quoting the following words of our Lord Jesus: "Come unto Me, all ye that labour and are heavy laden, and I will give you rest;" and, "The blood of Jesus Christ God's Son, cleanseth us from all sin." Then in a sentence or two he prayed fervently that the Holy Spirit might apply these words.

John had a suspicion that his mate was on the verge of a serious illness, and he was not wrong. Next day, Dorkin was stricken with a raging fever, and John Potter had not only to nurse him day and night, but to give constant attention to the lantern as well. Fortunately, the day after that the relief boat would be out, so he consoled himself with that thought; but the gale, which had been blowing for some days, increased that night until it blew a perfect hurricane. The sea round the Eddystone became a tremendous whirlpool of foam, and all hope of communication with the shore was cut off. Of course the unfortunate lighthouse-keeper hung out a signal of distress, although he knew full well that it could not be replied to.

Meanwhile a wedding party assembled in Plymouth. The bride was blooming and young; the bridegroom—strong and happy; but there was a shade upon his brow as he approached a stout elderly female, and said, sadly, "I can't tell you, mother, how grieved I am that father is not with us to-day. I would be quite willing to put it off, and so would Nora, for a few days, but there is no appearance of the storm abating; and, indeed, if even it stopped this moment, I don't think the relief-boat could get off in less than a week."

"I know it, Tommy." (It seemed ridiculous to call a strapping, curly-haired, bewhiskered, six-foot man "Tommy"!) "I know it, Tommy; but it ain't of no use puttin' of it off. I've always 'ad a settled conviction that anythink as is put off is as good as given up altogether. No, no, my son; go on with the weddin'."

So the wedding went on, and Nora Vining, a dark-haired Plymouth maiden, became Mrs Thomas Potter; and the breakfast was eaten, and the healths were drunk, and the speeches made, and Mrs Potter, senior, wept profusely (for joy) nearly all the time, into a white cotton handkerchief, which was so large and strong that some of the guests entertained the belief to the end of their lives that the worthy woman had had it manufactured for her own special use on that great occasion.

Meanwhile the father, whose absence was regretted so much, and whose heart would have rejoiced so much to have been there, remained in his lonely dwelling, out among the mad whirlpools in the wildest past of the raging sea. All day, and every day, his signal of distress streamed horizontally in the furious gale, and fishermen stood on the shore and wondered what was wrong, and wished so earnestly that the gale would go down; but no one, not even the boldest among them all, imagined for a moment that a boat could venture to leave the shore, much less encounter the seething billows on the Eddystone. As each night drew on, one by one the lights glimmered out above the rock, until the bright beams of the fully illuminated lantern poured like a flood through the murky air, and then men went home to their firesides, relieved to know that, whatever might be wrong, the keepers were at all events able to attend to their important duties.

Day after day Isaac Dorkin grew worse: he soon became delirious, and, strong though he was, John Potter was scarcely able to hold him down in bed. When the delirium first came on, John chanced to be in the lantern just commencing to light up. When he was about to apply the light, he heard a noise behind him, and, turning hastily round, beheld the flushed face and blazing eyes of his mate rising through the trap door that communicated with the rooms below. Leaving his work, John hastened to his friend, and with some difficulty persuaded him to return to his bed; but no sooner had he got him into it and covered him up, than a new paroxysm came on, and the sick man arose in the strength of his agony and hurled his friend to the other side of the apartment. John sprang up, and grappled with him while he was rushing towards the door. It was an awful struggle that ensued. Both were large and powerful men; the one strong in a resolute purpose to meet boldly a desperate case, the other mad with fever. They swayed to and fro, and fell on and smashed the homely furniture of the place; sometimes the one and sometimes the other prevailing, while both gasped for breath and panted vehemently; suddenly Dorkin sank down exhausted. He appeared to collapse, and John lifted him with difficulty again into his bed; but in a few seconds he attempted to renew the struggle, while the whole building was filled with his terrific cries.

While this was going on, the shades of night had been falling fast, and John Potter remembered that none of the candles had been lit, and that in a few minutes more the rock would be a source of greater danger to shipping than if no lighthouse had been there, because vessels would be making for the light from all quarters of the world, in the full faith of its being kept up! Filled with horror at the thought that perhaps even at that moment vessels might be hurrying on to their doom, he seized a piece of rope that lay at hand, and managed to wind it so firmly round his mate as to render him helpless. Bounding back to the lantern, he quickly lighted it up, but did not feel his heart relieved until he had gazed out at the snowy billows below, and made sure that no vessel was in view. Then he took a long draught of water, wiped his brow, and returned to his friend.

Two days after that Isaac Dorkin died. And now John Potter found himself in a more horrible situation than before. The storm continued: no sooner did one gale abate than another broke out, so as to render approach to the rock impossible; while, day after day, and night after night, the keeper had to pass the dead body of his mate several times in attending to the duties of the lantern. And still the signal of distress continued to fly from the lighthouse, and still the people on shore continued to wonder what was wrong, to long for moderate weather, and to feel relief when they saw the faithful light beam forth each evening at sunset.

At last the corpse began to decay, and John felt that it was necessary to get rid of it, but he dared not venture to throw it into the sea. It was well known that Dorkin had been a quarrelsome man, and he feared that if he could not produce the body when the relief came, he might be deemed a *murderer*. He therefore let it lie until it became so overpoweringly offensive that the whole building, from foundation to cupola, was filled with the horrible stench. The feelings of the solitary man can neither be conceived nor described. Well was it for John that he had the Word of God in his hand, and the grace of God in his heart during that awful period.

For nearly a month his agony lasted. At last the weather moderated. The boat came off; the "relief" was effected; and poor Dorkin's body, which was in such a condition that it could not be carried on shore, was thrown into the sea. Then John Potter returned home, and left the lighthouse service for ever.

From that time forward it has been the custom to station not fewer than three men at a time on all out-lying lighthouses of the kingdom.

Note. Reader, we have not drawn here on our imagination. This story is founded on unquestionable fact.

Chapter Six.

The End of Rudyerd's Lighthouse.

Thirty-Four years passed away, and still Rudyerd's lighthouse stood firm as the rock on which it was founded. True, during that period it had to undergo occasional repairs, because the timber uprights at the base, where exposed to the full violence of the waves, had become weather-worn, and required renewing in part; but this was only equivalent to a ship being overhauled and having some of her planks renewed. The main fabric of the lighthouse remained as sound and steadfast at the end of that long period as it was at the beginning, and it would in all probability have remained on the Eddystone Rock till the present day, had not a foe assailed it, whose nature was very different indeed from that with which it had been built to contend.

The lighthouse was at this time in charge of Teddy Maroon: not the Teddy who had bewailed his fate so disconsolately in the French prison in days gone by, but his youngest son, who was now getting to be an elderly man. We may, however, relieve the mind of the sympathetic reader, by saying that Teddy, senior, was not dead. He was still alive and hearty; though bent nearly double with extreme age; and dwelt on the borders of one of the Irish bogs, at the head of an extensive colony of Maroons.

One night Teddy the younger ascended to the lantern to trim the candles; he snuffed them all round and returned to the kitchen to have a pipe, his two mates being a-bed at the time. No one now knows how the thing happened, but certain it is that Teddy either dropped some of the burning snuff on the floor, or in some other way introduced more light into his lantern that night than it had ever been meant to contain, so that while he and his mates were smoking comfortably below, the lighthouse was smoking quietly, but ominously, above.

On shore, late that night, an elderly gentleman stood looking out of the window of a charmingly situated cottage in the village of Cawsand Bay, near Plymouth, which commanded a magnificent prospect of the channel.

"Father," he said, turning to a very old man seated beside the fire, who, although shrunken and wrinkled and bald, was ruddy in complexion, and evidently in the enjoyment of a green old age, "Father, the lighthouse is beautifully bright to-night; shall I help you to the window to look at it?"

"Yes, Tommy: I'm fond o' the old light. It minds me of days gone by, when you and I were young, Martha."

The old man gave a chuckle as he looked across the hearthstone, where, in a chair similar to his own, sat a very stout and very deaf and very old lady, smoothing the head of her grandchild, a little girl, who was the youngest of a family of ten.

Old Martha did not hear John Potter's remark, but she saw his kindly smile, and nodded her head with much gravity in reply. Martha had grown intellectually slow when she partially lost her hearing, and although she was not sad she had evidently become solemn. An English Dictionary and the Bible were the only books that Martha would look at now. She did not use the former as a help to the understanding of the latter. No one knew why she was so partial to the dictionary; but as she not unfrequently had it on her knee upside down while poring over it, her grandchild, little Nora, took up the idea that she had resolved to devote the latter days of her life to learning to read backwards! Perhaps the fact that the dictionary had once belonged to her son James who was wrecked and drowned on the Norfolk coast, may have had something to do with it.

With the aid of his son's arm and a stick old John managed to hobble to the window.

"It is very bright. Why, Tommy," he exclaimed, with a start, "it's too bright: the lighthouse must be on fire!"

At that moment, "Tommy's" wife, now "fat, fair, and *fifty*" (or thereabouts), entered the room hurriedly, exclaiming, "Oh, Tom, what *can* be the matter with the lighthouse, I never saw it so bright before?"

Tom, who had hastily placed his father in a chair, so that he could see the Eddystone, seized his hat, and exclaiming, "I'll go and see, my dear," ran out and proceeded to the shore.

"What's the matter?" cried Mrs Potter in a querulous voice, when little Nora rushed from her side.

Nora, senior, went to her at once, and, bending down, said, in a musical voice that retained much of its clearness and all its former sweetness: "I fear that the lighthouse is on fire, grandma!"

Mrs Potter gazed straight before her with vacant solemnity, and Nora, supposing that she had not heard, repeated the information.

Still Mrs Potter made no reply; but, after a few moments, she turned her eyes on her daughter-in-law with owlish gravity, and said; "I knew it! I said long ago to your father, my dear, I had a settled conviction that that lighthouse would come to a bad end."

It did indeed appear as though old Martha's prophecy were about to come true!

Out at the lighthouse Teddy Maroon, having finished his pipe, went up to the lantern to trim the candles again. He had no sooner opened the hatch of the lantern than a dense cloud of smoke burst out. He shouted to his comrades, one of whom, Henry Hall, was old and not fit for much violent exertion; the other, James Wilkie, was a young man, but a heavy sleeper. They could not be roused as quickly as the occasion demanded. Teddy ran to the store-room for a leathern bucket, but before he could descend to the rock, fill it and re-ascend, the flames had got a firm hold of the cupola. He dashed the water into the lantern just as his horrified comrades appeared.

"Fetch bucketfulls as fast as ye can. Och, be smart, boys, if iver ye was," he shouted, while perspiration streamed down his face. Pulling off his coat, while his mates ran down for water, Teddy dashed wildly into the lantern, and, holding the coat by its arms, laid about him violently, but smoke and fire drove him but almost immediately. The buckets were long of coming, and when they did arrive, their contents were as nothing on the glowing cupola. Then Teddy went out on the balcony and endeavoured to throw the water up, but the height was too great. While he was doing this, Wilkie ran down for more water, but Hall stood gazing upwards, open-mouthed with horror, at the raging flames. At that moment the leaden covering of the roof melted, and rushed down on Hall's head and shoulders. He fell, with a loud shriek. While Teddy tried to drag him down to the room below, he exclaimed that some of the melted lead had gone down his throat! He was terribly burned about the neck, but his comrades had to leave him in his bed while they strove wildly to check the flames. It was all in vain. The wood-work around the lantern, from years of exposure to the heat of twenty-four large candles burning at once, had become like tinder, and the fire became so fierce that the timber courses composing the top of the column soon caught. Then the keepers saw that any further efforts would be useless. The great exertions made to carry up even a few bucketsfull of water soon exhausted their strength, and they were driven from room to room as the fire descended. At last the heat and smoke became so intense that they were driven out of the lighthouse altogether, and sought shelter in a cavern or hollow under the ladder, on the east side of the rock. Fortunately it was low water at the time, and the weather was calm. Had it been otherwise, the rock would have been no place of refuge.

Meanwhile Mr Thomas Potter (our old friend Tommy—now, as we have said an elderly gentleman) went off in a large boat with a crew of stout fishermen from Cawsand Bay, having a smaller boat in tow. When they reached the rock, a terrific spectacle was witnessed. The lighthouse was enveloped in flames nearly to the bottom, for the outside planking, being caulked and covered with pitch, was very inflammable. The top glowed against the dark sky and looked in the midst of the smoke like a fiery meteor. The Eddystone Rock was suffused with a dull red light, as if it were becoming red hot, and the surf round it appeared to hiss against the fire, while in the dark shadow of the cave the three lighthouse keepers were seen cowering in terror,—as they well might, seeing that melted lead and flaming masses of wood and other substances were falling thickly round them.

To get them out of their dangerous position was a matter of extreme difficulty, because, although there was little or no wind, the swell caused a surf on the rock which absolutely forbade the attempt to land. In this emergency they fell upon a plan which seemed to afford some hope of success. They anchored the large boat to the westward, and veered down towards the rock as far as they dared venture. Then three men went into the small boat, which was eased off and sent farther in by means of a rope. When as near as it was possible to approach, a coil of rope was thrown to the rock. It was caught by Teddy Maroon, and although in extreme danger and anxiety, the men in the boat could not help giving vent to a ringing cheer. Teddy at once tied the end of the rope round the waist of old Henry Hall, and half persuaded, half forced him into the surf, through which he was hauled into the boat in safety. Wilkie went next, and Teddy followed. Thus they were rescued, put on board the large boat, and carried on shore; but no sooner did the keel grate on the sand, than Wilkie, who had never spoken a word, and who appeared half stupefied, bounded on shore and ran off at full speed. It is a curious fact, which no one has ever been able to account for, that this man was never more heard of! As it is quite certain that he did not cause the fire, and also that he did his utmost to subdue it, the only conclusion that could be come to was, that the excitement and terror had driven him mad. At all events that was the last of him.

Another curious fact connected with the fire is, that Henry Hall actually did swallow a quantity of melted lead. He lingered for twelve days after the accident, and then died. Afterwards his body was opened, and an oval lump of lead, which weighed upwards of seven ounces, was found in his stomach. This extraordinary fact is authenticated by the credible testimony of a respectable medical man and several eye-witnesses.

Meanwhile, the lighthouse continued to burn, despite the most strenuous efforts made to save it. Had a storm arisen, the seas would speedily have quenched the fire, but unfortunately the weather continued fine and comparatively calm for several days, while the wind was just strong enough to fan the fury of the flames, and at the same time to cause a surf sufficiently high to render a landing on the rock impossible. But, indeed, even if this had been effected, the efforts that could have been made with the small fire-engines at that time in use, would have been utterly useless. The fire gradually descended to the different courses of solid timber, the well-hole of the staircase assisting the draught, and the outside timbers and inside mast, or wooden core, forming a double connecting link whereby the devouring element was carried to the very bottom of the building, with a heat so intense that the courses of Cornish moor-stone were made red hot.

Admiral West, with part of the fleet, happened to be at that time in Plymouth Sound. He at once sent a sloop with a fire-engine to the rock. They attempted to land in a boat, but could not. So violent was the surf, that the boat was at one time thrown bodily upon the rock by one wave and swept off again by the next. The escape on this occasion was almost miraculous, the men therefore did not venture to make another attempt, but contented themselves with endeavouring to work the engine from the boat, in doing which they broke it, and thus all hope of doing anything further was gone. But indeed the engine they had would have availed nothing, even though it had been twice as powerful, against such a mighty conflagration. As well might they have tried to extinguish Vesuvius with a tea-kettle!

For four days and nights did that massive pillar of fire burn. At last it fell in ruins before the most irresistible element with which man or matter has to contend, after having braved the fury of the winds and waves for nearly half a century.

Thus perished the second lighthouse that was built on the Eddystone Rock, in December of the year 1755, and thus, once again, were those black reefs left unguarded. Once more that dread of mariners, ancient and modern, became a trap on the south coast of England—a trap now rendered doubly dangerous by the fact that, for so long a period, ships had been accustomed to make for it instead of avoiding it, in the full expectation of receiving timely warning from its friendly light.

Chapter Seven.

Old Friends In New Circumstances.

We open the story of the third, and still existing, lighthouse on the Eddystone with the re-introduction of Teddy Maroon—that Teddy who acted so prominent a part at the burning of Rudyerd's tower in December 1755.

Men's activities seem to have been quickened at this period of time, for only about six months were allowed to elapse between the destruction of the old and the commencement of operations for the new lighthouse.

It was a calm evening in the autumn 1756 when Teddy Maroon, smoking a little black pipe, sauntered towards the residence of old John Potter. On reaching the door he extinguished the little pipe by the summary process of thrusting the point of his blunt forefinger into the bowl, and deposited it hot in his vest pocket. His tap was answered by a small servant girl, with a very red and ragged head of hair, who ushered him into the presence of the aged couple. They were seated in the two chairs—one on each side of the fireplace—which they might almost be said to inhabit. Little Nora was stirring a few embers of coal into a cheery flame, for she knew the old people loved the sight of the fire even in summer. On a chair beside old Martha lay the open Bible, from which Nora had been reading, and on old Martha's knee was the valued dictionary, upside down as usual.

"Glad to see you, lad," said old John, with a pleasant smile as he extended his hand; "it does us good to see you; it minds us so of old times."

"Ah, then, I've got to tell 'ee what'll mind you more of owld times than the mere sight o' me face," said Teddy, as he patted old Martha on the shoulder and sat down beside her. "How are 'ee, owld ooman?"

"Ay," replied Martha in a tremulous voice, "you're uncommon like your father—as like as two peas."

"Faix, av ye saw the dear owld gintleman now," said Teddy with a laugh, "ye'd think there was a difference. Hows'ever, its o' no use repaitin' me question, for any man could see that you're in the best o' health—you're bloomin' like a cabbage rose."

The latter part of this complimentary speech was shouted into old Martha's ear, and she responded by shaking her head and desiring the flatterer to "go along."

"Well, John," said the visitor, turning to his father's old friend, "you'll be glad to hear that I've been engaged to work at the new lighthouse, an', moreover we've got fairly begun."

"You *don't* say so," cried John Potter, with some of the old fire sparkling in his eyes; "well, now, that is pleasant noos. Why, it makes me a'most wish to be young again. Of course I heard that they've bin hard at the preparations for a good while; but few people comes to see me now; they think I'm too old to be interested in anything; I suppose; an' I didn't know that it was fairly begun, or that you were on the work: I'd like to hear what your old father would say to it, Teddy."

"I don't know what he'd say to it," responded the Irishman, "but I know what he threatens to do, for I wrote him the other day tellin' him all about it, an' he bade my sister Kathleen write back that he's more nor half a mind to come and superintend the operations."

"What is it all about, Nora?" demanded old Martha, who had been gazing intently at her husband's countenance during the conversation.

Nora put her pretty lips to her grandmother's ear and gave the desired information, whereupon the old lady looked solemnly at her spouse, and laying her hand on the dictionary, said, with strong though quivering emphasis: "now, John, mark my words, I 'ave a settled conviction that that light'ouse will come to a bad end. It's sure to be burnt or blow'd over."

Having given vent to which prophecy, she relapsed into herself and appeared to ruminate on it with peculiar satisfaction.

"And what's the name of the architect?" demanded John.

"Smeaton," replied Teddy Maroon.

"Never heerd of 'im before," returned John.

"No more did I," said Teddy.

The two friends appeared to find food for meditation in this point of ignorance, for they fell into a state of silence for a few minutes, which was interrupted by the sudden entrance of Mr Thomas Potter. He looked a little wearied as he sat down beside his mother, whose face lighted up with an expression of intense delight as she said, "Come away, Tommy, where have you been, my boy?"

"I've been out on the sea, mother, after mischief as usual," replied Tommy, whose bald head and wrinkled brow repudiated, while his open hearty smile appeared to justify, the juvenile name.

"What! they 'aven't engaged you on the noo light'ouse, 'ave they?" said old Martha, in horror.

"No, no, mother, don't fear that," said her son, hastening to relieve her mind, "but you know the new engineer is gathering information from all quarters, and he naturally applied to me, because I am of his own profession and have known and studied the rock since I was a little boy."

"Know'd an' studied it," exclaimed Martha with more than her wonted vigour, "ay, an' if you'd said you'd a'most broke your old mother's heart with it, you'd 'ave said no more than the truth, Tommy. It's a wonder as that rock hasn't brought me to a prematoor grave. However, it ain't likely to do so now, an' I'm glad they have not inveigled you into it, my boy; for it's an awful place for wettin' of your feet an' dirt'in' of your hands and pinafores, an'—"

The old lady, relapsing here into early reminiscences, once more retired within herself, while. Teddy Maroon and John Potter, mentioning their ignorance as to the architect who had undertaken the great work, demanded of "Mister Thomas" if he could enlighten them.

"Of course I can," he replied, "for he is well known to his friends as a most able man, and will become better known to the world, if I may venture to prophesy, as the builder of what is sure to be the most famous lighthouse on the English coast. His name is Smeaton, and he is not an engineer."

"Not an engineer?" echoed Teddy and old John, in surprise.

"No, he's a mathematical instrument maker."

"Well now," said John Potter, gazing meditatively into the fireplace where Nora had evoked a tiny flame, "that is strange. This Eddystun Rock seems to have what I may call a pecooliar destiny. The builder of the first light'ouse was a country gentleman; of the second, a silk-mercer; and now, as you say, the third is to be put up by a maker o' mathymatical instruments. I only hope," continued John, shaking his head gravely at the fireplace, "that he won't make a mess of it like the others did."

"Come now, father," returned his son, "don't say that the others made a mess of it. We must remember that Winstanley began his building in what we may call total darkness. No other man before him had attempted such a work, so that he had no predecessor whose good points he might imitate, or whose failures he might avoid. Many a trained engineer might have made a worse mess of it, and, to my mind, it says much for poor Winstanley's capacity, all things considered, that his lighthouse stood so long as the six or seven years of its building. Then as to Rudyerd's one, it was in reality a great success. It stood firm for nigh fifty years, and, but for the fire, might have stood for any number of years to come. It cannot be justly said that he made a mess of it. As well might you say that the builders of a first-rate ship made a mess of it because someone set her alight after she had sailed the ocean for half a century."

"True, Tommy, true," said old John, nodding acquiescence emphatically. On seeing this, old Martha, knowing nothing about the matter because of her deafness, nodded emphatically also, and said, "that's so, Tommy, I always 'ad a settled conviction that you was right, except," she added, as if to guard herself, "except w'en you was after mischief."

"Well, but Tommy," continued old John, "you was agoin' to tell us somethin' about this Mister Smeaton. What sort of a man is he?"

"As far as I can judge, on short acquaintance," replied Potter, "he seems to be a man who has got a mind and a will of his own, and looks like one who won't be turned out of his straight course by trifles. His name is John, which is a good bible name, besides being yours, father, and he comes from Leeds, a highly respectable place, which has produced men of note before now. His age is thirty-two, which is about the most vigorous period of a man's life, and he has come to his present business in spite of all opposition, a fact which is favourable to the prospects of the lighthouse. In short he's a natural genius, and a born engineer. His father, an attorney, wished him to follow his own profession, but it was soon clear that that was out of the question, for the boy's whole soul was steeped from earliest childhood in mechanics."

"I once knew a boy," said John Potter, with a smile, "whose whole soul was steeped in the same thing!"

"And in mischief," added old Martha, suddenly, much to every one's surprise. The old woman's deafness was indeed of a strangely intermittent type!

"Well," continued Potter, with a laugh and a nod to his mother, "no doubt Smeaton had a spice of mischief in him among other qualities, for it is said of him that when quite a little fellow he made a force pump, with which he emptied his father's fish-pond of water, to the detriment, not to say consternation, of the fish. The upshot of it all was that the lad was apprenticed to a maker of mathematical instruments, and soon proved himself to be an inventive genius of considerable power. Ere long he commenced business on his own account, and has now undertaken the task of building the *third* lighthouse on the Eddystone. I was in London lately, and saw the beautiful models of the intended structure which Smeaton has made with his own hands, and it seems to me that he's just the man to do the work."

At the mention of models, old John Potter's eyes lighted up, for it brought the memory of former days vividly before him.

"He means to build it of stone," said the son.

"Stone, say 'ee? that's right, Tommy, that's right," said old John, with a nod of strong approval, "I've always thought that the weak point in the old light'ouses was *want of weight*. On such a slope of a foundation, you know, it requires great weight to prevent the seas washin' a lighthouse clean away."

"I've thought the same thing, father, but what you and I only thought of Smeaton has stated, and intends to act upon. He means to build a tower so solid that it will defy the utmost fury of winds and waves. He is going to cut the sloping foundation into a series of steps or shelves, which will prevent the possibility of slipping. The shape of the building is to be something like the trunk of an oak tree, with a wider base than the lighthouse of Rudyerd. The first twenty feet or so of it is to be built solid; each stone to be made in the shape of a dovetail, and all the stones circling round a central key to which they will cling, as well as to each other, besides being held by bolts and cement, so that the lower part of the building will be as firm as the rock on which it stands. But I daresay, father," continued his son, with a glance at Teddy Maroon, "our friend here, being engaged on the work, has told you all about this already."

"Not I," said Maroon, quickly, "I've bin too busy to come here until to-day, and though I've got me own notions o' what Mr Smeaton intends, by obsarvin' what's goin' on, I han't guessed the quarter o' what you've towld me, sur. Howsever, I can spake to what's bin already done. You must know," said Teddy, with a great affectation of being particular, "Mr Smeaton has wisely secured his workmen by howldin' out pleasant prospects to 'em. In the first place, we've got good regular wages, an' additional pay whin we're on the Rock. In the second place, extra work on shore is paid for over an' above the fixed wages. In the third place, each man has got his appinted dooty, an's kep close at it. In the fourth place, the rules is uncommon stringent, and instant dismissal follers the breakin' of 'em. In the fifth place—"

"Never mind the fifth place, Teddy," interrupted old John, "like yer father, ye was ever too fond o' waggin' yer tongue. Just tell us straight off, if ye can, what's been already done at the Rock."

"Well, well," said Maroon, with a deprecatory smile, "owld father an' me's always bin misonderstud more or less; but no matter. Av coorse we've had the usual difficulties to fight agin, for the owld Eddystone Rock ain't agoin' to change its natur to please nobody. As me father described it in *his* day, so I finds it in mine. On most of our first visits we got wet skins; but little or no work done, for though it might be ever so calm here at Plymouth, it always seemed to be blowin' a private gale out at the Rock—leastwise, av it warn't blowin', there was swell enough most days to make the landin' troublesome. So we got wan hour's work at wan time, an' two hours, or may be three, at another, off an' on. As the saison advanced we got on better, sometimes got five and six hours on the Rock right on ind, and whin the tide sarved we wint at it by torch-light. Wan week we got no less than sixty-four an' a half hours on it, an' we was all in great sperrits intirely over that, for you see, mister Potter, we're all picked men an' takes a pride in the work—to say nothin' of havin' a good master. Av coorse we've had the usual botherations wid the sharp rocks cuttin' the cable of our attendin'-sloop, an' gales suddinly gettin' up whin we was at the Rock wantin' to land, as well as suddinly goin' down whin we wasn't at the Rock, so that we missed our chances. But such sorrows was what we expicted, more or less. The wust disappointment we've had has bin wi' the noo store-ship, the *Neptune Buss*. I wish it was the Neptune *bu'st*, I do, for it's wus than a tub, an' gives us more trouble than it's all worth. Now the saison's drawin' to a close, it's clear that we'll do no more this year than cut the foundations."

"An' that's not a bad season's work, lad," said old John. "Ain't it not, Tommy?"

"Not bad, indeed, father, for there are always unusual and vexatious delays at the beginning of a great work; besides, some of the greatest difficulties in connexion with such buildings are encountered in the preparation of the foundations. I suppose Mr Smeaton means to dress the stones on shore, ready for laying?" continued Potter the younger, turning to Maroon, who had risen and was buttoning up his monkey-jacket.

"Why, yes sur, haven't you bin down at the yard?"

"Not yet. I've only just arrived in town; and must be off again to-morrow. You can't think how disappointed I am at being prevented by business from taking part in the building of the new lighthouse—"

"What's that you say, Tommy?" interrupted old Martha, putting her hand to her ear and wrinkling her brow interrogatively.

"That I'm grieved, mother, at not being able to help in building the new lighthouse," shouted her son, in a voice that might have split an ordinary ear.

Old Martha's visage relaxed into a faint smile as she turned towards the fire and looked earnestly at it, as if for explanation or consolation.

"Ay ay," she muttered, "it would have bin strange if you hadn't wished that; you was always up to mischief, Tommy; always; or else wishin' to be up to it, although you might know as well as I know myself, that if you did get leave to go hout to the Rock (which you're for ever wantin' to do), it would be wet feet an dirty pinafores mornin', noon, an' night, which it's little you care for that, you bad boy, though it causes me no end of washin' an' dryin',—ay ay!"

The old woman looked up in the smiling countenance of her stalwart son, and becoming apparently a little confused by reminiscences of the past and evidences of the present, retired within herself and relapsed into silence.

"Well, sur," continued Teddy, "just give a look down if you can; it's worth your while. Mr Smeaton means to have every stone cut in the yard here on shore, and to lay down each 'course' in the yard too, to be sure that it all fits, for we'll have no time out at the Rock to correct mistakes or make alterations. It'll be 'sharp's the word, boys, and look alive O!' all through; ship the stones; off to the Rock; land 'em in hot haste; clap on the cement; down wi' the blocks; work like blazes—or Irishmen, which is much the same thing; make all fast into the boats again; sailors shoutin' 'Look alive, me hearties! squall bearin' down right abaft of the lee stuns'l gangway!'—or somethin' like that; up sail, an' hooroo! boys, for the land, weather permittin'; if not, out to say an' take things aisy, or av ye can't be aisy, be as aisy as ye can!"

"A pleasant prospect, truly," said Mr T. Potter, laughing, as he shook the Irishman's horny hand.

"Good-bye, John. Good-bye, Nora, me darlin'; Good-bye, owld ooman."

"Hold your noise, lad," said old Martha, looking gravely into her visitor's face.

"That's just what I manes to do, mavoorneen," replied Teddy Maroon, with a pleasant nod, "for I'll be off to the Rock to-morrow by day-break, weather permittin', an' it's little help any noise from me would give to the waves that kape gallivantin' wid the reefs out there like mad things, from Sunday to Saturday, all the year round."

When the door shut on the noisy Irishman, it seemed as though one of the profound calms so much needed and desired out at the Eddystone Rock had settled down in old John Potter's home—a calm which was not broken for some minutes thereafter except by old Martha muttering softly once or twice, while she gravely shook her head: "Hold your noise, Teddy, hold your noise, lad; you're very like your father; hold your noise!"

Chapter Eight.

Experiences, Difficulties, and Dangers of the First Season.

While the building of the new lighthouse was being thus calmly discussed on shore, out at the Eddystone the wild waves were lashing themselves into fierce fury, as if they had got wind of what was being done, and had hurried from all ends of the sea to interdict proceedings. In hurrying to the field of battle these wild waves indulged in a little of their favourite pastime. They caught up two unfortunate vessels—a large West Indiaman and a man-of-war's tender—and bore them triumphantly towards the fatal Rock. It seemed as though the waves regarded these as representative vessels, and meant thus to cast the royal and the merchant navies on the Eddystone, by way, as it were, of throwing down the gauntlet to presumptuous Man.

For want of the famous light the vessels bore straight down upon the Rock, and the wild waves danced and laughed, and displayed their white teeth and their seething ire, as if in exultation at the thought of the shattered hulls and mangled corpses, which they hoped ere long to toss upon their crests.

Fortunately, Man was on the "look out!" The *Buss* was tugging at her moorings off the Rock, and some of the seamen and hands were perambulating the deck, wishing for settled weather, and trying to pierce the gloom by which they were surrounded. Suddenly the two vessels were seen approaching. The alarm was given. Those on board the doomed ships saw their danger when too late, and tried to sheer off the fatal spot, but their efforts were fruitless. The exulting waves hurried them irresistibly on. In this extremity the Eddystone men leaped into their yawl, pushed off, and succeeded in towing both vessels out of danger; at once demonstrating the courage of English hearts and the need there was for English hands to complete the work on which they were then engaged.

Next day Mr Smeaton came off to visit the Rock, and the news of the rescue served him for a text on which to preach a lay-sermon as to the need of every man exerting himself to the uttermost in a work which was so obviously a matter of life and death. It was, however, scarcely necessary to urge these men, for they were almost all willing. But not all; in nearly every flock there is a black sheep or so, that requires weeding out. There were two such sheep among the builders of the Eddystone. Being good at everything, Smeaton was a good weeder. He soon had them up by the roots and cast out. A foreman proved to be disorderly, and tried to make the men promise, "that if he should be discharged they would all follow him." Smeaton at once assembled the men and gave orders that such of them as had any dependence on, or attachment to, the refractory foreman, should take up his tools and follow him. Only one did so—the rest stood firm.

At this time the weather was very unsettled, and the work progressed slowly. Once or twice it was still further retarded, by men who should have known better, in the following manner:

One evening one of the lighthouse boats was boarded by a cutter, the officer in charge of which proceeded to "impress" several of the men into the navy.

"It's to be pressed we are," murmured Teddy Maroon to one of his mates, in a vexed tone, "sure the tater-heads might know we've got an Admiralty protection."

Whether the officer knew this or not, it was evident that he had overheard the remark, for, after selecting two of the best men, he turned, and, pointing to Maroon, said aloud:—

"Let that tater-head also jump on board. He's not worth much, but the service is in want of powder-monkeys just now. Perhaps he'll do. If not, I'll send him back."

Thus was the poor Irishman carried off with his two mates to fight the battles of his country! In a few days, however, they were all sent back, and the indiscreet officer who had impressed them got a reprimand for his pains. After the first season they had no further interruptions from this source.

Large mainsails were given them for their boats, with a lighthouse painted on each, and every man obtained besides a silver medal of exemption from impressment.

But this was only the commencement of poor Teddy's "throubles" at that time. He had scarcely returned to his work when a new one overtook him. This was, however, in the way of business.

"Teddy, my fine fellow," said Richardson, the foreman, as they stood on the deck of the *Buss* holding on to the mizzen shrouds, "it's quite clear to me that with the wind dead against them like this, the relief boat with Hill's company won't be able to get off, and as we're short of provisions, I mean to take the big yawl and go ashore with my gang. As the best men are always chosen for posts of danger, I shall leave you in charge of the *Buss* with two hands—Smart and Bowden;—both stanch fellows as you know."

"I'm your servant, sir," said Teddy, "only if the best men are wanted here, hadn't you better stop yourself, an' I'll take the rest ashore?"

Richardson did not see his way to this, though he acknowledged the compliment, and that evening Teddy found himself in command of the despised *Buss*, with half a gale blowing, and, as he observed, "more where that came from."

Teddy was right, "more" did come, and kept him and his mates idle prisoners for a week. Indeed the whole of that month had been so stormy that from the 16th to the 30th only twenty hours' work had been done on the Rock.

During six days the three men stuck to their post, but at the end of that time Teddy called a council of war.

"Gintlemen," said he, "(for men in our pursition must be purlite to sich other), it's our dooty to stick by this here tub so long's it's of any use to do so; but as she seems to be well able to look after herself, an' our purvisions has come down to the last ounce, it's my opinion—founded on profound meditations over me last pipe—that we'd better go ashore."

To this speech John Bowden replied "I'm agreeable, for it's not my dooty to starve myself."

William Smart, however, intimated that he was "*dis*agreeable."

"Because," said he, "its blowin' great guns, an' looks as if it meant to go on, which is not a state of weather suitable for goin' over a dozen miles of sea in a small open boat, without even a mast or a rag of sail to bless herself with."

"Pooh!" exclaimed Maroon, contemptuously; "a blanket'll make the best of sails."

"Ay," added Bowden, "and an oar will do well enough for a mast—anyhow we'll try, for most votes carry in all well-regulated meetin's."

This plan, although attended with considerable danger, was finally agreed to, and forthwith acted on.

That afternoon the men on shore observed a very Robinson-Crusoe-like boat coming in from the sea with an oar-mast and a blanket-sail, from which landed "Captain" Teddy Maroon and his two mates. The same evening, however, the wind moderated and shifted a little, so that the relief boat, with provisions and the gang of men whose turn it was to do duty in the store-ship, succeeded in getting off and reaching their *Buss* in safety.

The weather became so bad soon after this that Smeaton thought it wise to bring his operations for that season to a close. Accordingly, on the 7th November, he visited the Rock, which had been cut into a regular floor of successive terraces or steps, and was considerably larger in circumference than the foundation on which Rudyerd's building had rested. On the 15th the *Buss* sailed into Plymouth, the men having run out of provisions, and having been unable to do anything on the Rock.

A great storm raged on the 22nd. On the previous day Smeaton had gone off in the *Buss* to attach a buoy to the mooring chains for that winter. The task was laborious, and when it was completed they found it impossible to return to Plymouth, owing to the miserable sailing qualities of their vessel. There was nothing for it but to cast loose and run before the wind. While doing so they snapt the painter of the yawl, and lost it.

Thus they were, as it were, cast adrift upon the sea with neither maps, charts, books, nor instruments to guide them. No alarm, however, was felt, the neighbouring headlands being bold, and all on board having previously been at Fowey, to which port Smeaton now gave orders to steer.

Wet and worn out with labour, he then went below to snatch a few hours' repose. In the night he was awakened by a tremendous noise overhead. The men were rushing about the deck, and shouting wildly. He sprang up without dressing. A voice, exclaiming, "For God's sake heave hard on that rope if you want to save yourselves!" saluted him as he gained the deck. Roaring wind, a deluge of rain, and pitch darkness held revel on the sea; but above the din was heard the dreaded sound of breakers close under their lee. The jib was split, the mainsail half-lowered, and the vessel running gunwale under. By vigorous and well-directed action, in which John Bowden proved himself to be one of those men who are towers of strength in emergencies, the head of the *Buss* was brought round, and the immediate danger averted, but they had no idea where they were, and when day broke on the 23rd they found themselves out of sight of land! Their last boat, also, had filled while towing astern, and had to be cut adrift. At noon, however; they sighted the Land's End—the wind blowing hard from the nor'-east.

"No chance o' making a British port in this wind with such a vessel, sir," said John Bowden, touching his cap respectfully to Mr Smeaton.

"As well try to bate to win'ard in me grandmother's wash-tub," remarked Teddy Maroon, in a disrespectful tone.

Smeaton, agreeing with them, lay-to the whole of the 24th, and then, casting anchor, debated whether it were better to make for the coast of France or try to reach the Scilly Islands. Fortunately a change of wind on the 25th enabled them to weigh anchor and run back to Plymouth rejoicing; and vowing, as John Bowden said, never more to venture out to sea in a *Buss*! They reached the harbour at six in the morning, to the intense relief of their friends, who had given them up for lost.

Thus ended the first season—1756.

Chapter Nine.

Account of the War Continued.

"Now then, my lads," said Smeaton, on the 12th of June 1757, "we shall lay the foundation to-day, so let us go to work with a will."

"Faix, then," whispered Teddy Maroon to John Bowden, as they proceeded to the wharf, where the ready-cut stones were being put on board the Eddystone boat, "it's little good we'll do av we *don't* go to work wid a will."

"I believe you, my boy," replied John, heartily. John Bowden said and did everything heartily. "An' we won't be long," he continued, "about laying the first course, it's such a small one."

"Hallo!" shouted the man in charge of the boat, as they came in sight of it, "come along, lads; we're all ready."

According to directions they ran down, and jumped on board "with a will." Smeaton took his place in the stern. They pushed off with a will; sailed and pulled out the fourteen miles with a will; jumped on the rock, landed the heavy stones, went immediately into action, cleaned the bed, and laid the first stone of the great work—all under the same vigorous impulse of the will. This was at eight in the morning. By the evening tide, the first "course," which formed but a small segment of a circle, was fitted with the utmost despatch, bedded in mortar and trenailed down. Next day the second course was partly landed on the rock; the men still working with a will, for moments out there were more precious than hours or days in ordinary building,—but before they got the whole course landed, old Ocean also began to work with a will, and eventually proved himself stronger than his adversaries, by driving them, in a terrific storm, from the Rock!

They reached the *Buss* with difficulty, and lay there idle while the mad waves revelled round the rocks, and danced through their works deridingly. It seemed, however, as though they were only "in fun," for, on returning to work after the gale abated, it was found that "no harm had been done." As if, however, to check any premature felicitations, old Ocean again sent a sudden squall on the 18th, which drove the men once more off the rock, without allowing time to chain the stones landed, so that five of them were lost.

This was a serious disaster. The lost stones could only be replaced by new ones being cut from the distant quarries. Prompt in all emergencies, Smeaton hurried away and set two men to work on each stone, night and day; nevertheless, despite his utmost efforts, seconded by willing men, the incident caused the loss of more than a week.

Fogs now stepped in to aid and abet the winds and waves in their mad efforts to stop the work. Stop it! They little knew what indomitable spirits some men have got. As well might they have attempted to stop the course of time! They succeeded, however, in causing vexatious delays, and, in July, had the audacity to fling a wreck in the very teeth of the builders, as if to taunt them with the futility of their labours.

It happened thus: On the night of the 5th a vessel named the *Charming Sally*, about 130 tons burden, and hailing from Biddeford, came sailing over the main. A bright lookout was kept on board of her, of course, for the wind was moderately high, and the fog immoderately thick. The *Sally* progressed charmingly till midnight, when the look-out observed "something" right ahead. He thought the something looked like fishing-boats, and, being an unusually bright fellow, he resolved to wait until he should be quite sure before reporting what he saw. With a jovial swirl the waves bore the *Charming Sally* to her doom. "Rocks ahead!" roared the bright look-out, rather suddenly. "Rocks under her bottom," thought the crew of seven hands, as they leaped on deck, and felt the out-lying reefs of the Eddystone playing pitch and toss with their keel. Dire was the confusion on board, and cruel were the blows dealt with ungallant and unceasing violence at the hull of the *Charming Sally*; and black, black as the night would have been the fate of the hapless seamen on that occasion if the builders of the Eddystone had not kept a brighter look-out on board their sheltering *Buss*. John Bowden had observed the vessel bearing down on the rocks, and gave a startling alarm. Without delay a boat was launched and pulled to the rescue. Meanwhile the vessel filled so fast that their boat floated on the deck before the crew could get into it, and the whole affair had occurred so suddenly that some of the men, when taken off, were only in their shirts. That night the rescued men were hospitably entertained in the *Buss* by the builders of the new lighthouse, and, soon after, the ribs of the *Charming Sally* were torn to pieces by the far-famed teeth of the Eddystone—another added to the countless thousands of wrecks which had been demonstrating the urgent need there was for a lighthouse there, since the earliest days of navigation.

Having enacted this pleasant little episode, the indefatigable builders set to work again to do battle with the winds and waves. That the battle was a fierce one is incidentally brought out by the fact that on the 8th of August the sea was said "for the first time" to have refrained from going over the works during a whole tide!

On the 11th of the same month the building was brought to a level with the highest point of the Rock. This was a noteworthy epoch, inasmuch as the first completely *circular* course was laid down, and the men had more space to move about.

Mr Smeaton, indeed, seems to have moved about too much. Possibly the hilarious state of his mind unduly affected his usually sedate body. At all events, from whatever cause, he chanced to tumble off the edge of the building, and fell on the rocks below, at the very feet of the amazed Teddy Maroon, who happened to be at work there at the time.

"Och, is it kilt ye are, sur?" demanded the Irishman.

"Not quite," replied Smeaton, rising and carefully examining his thumb, which had been dislocated.

"Sure now it's a sargeon ye should have bin," said Teddy, as his commander jerked the thumb into its place as though it had been the disabled joint of a mathematical instrument, and quietly returned to his labours.

About this time also the great shears, by means of which the stones were raised to the top of the building, were overturned, and fell with a crash amongst the men; fortunately, however, no damage to life or limb resulted, though several narrow escapes were made. Being now on a good platform, they tried to work at night with the aid of links, but the enemy came down on them in the form of wind, and constantly blew the links out. The builders, determined not to be beaten, made a huge bonfire of their links. The enemy, growing furious, called up reinforcements of the waves, and not only drowned out the bonfire but drove the builders back to the shelter of their fortress, the *Buss*, and shut them up there for several days, while the waves, coming constantly up in great battalions, broke high over the re-erected shears, and did great damage to the machinery and works, but failed to move the sturdy root of the lighthouse which had now been fairly planted, though the attack was evidently made in force, this being the worst storm of the season. It lasted fifteen days.

On the 1st September the enemy retired for a little repose, and the builders, instantly sallying out, went to work again "with a will," and secured eighteen days of uninterrupted progress. Then the ocean, as if refreshed, renewed the attack, and kept it up with such unceasing vigour that the builders drew off and retired into winter quarters on the 3rd of October, purposing to continue the war in the following spring.

During this campaign of 1757 the column of the lighthouse had risen four feet six inches above the highest point of the Eddystone Rock. Thus ended the second season, and the wearied but dauntless men returned to the work-yard on shore to carve the needful stones, and otherwise to prepare ammunition for the coming struggle.

Sitting one night that winter at John Potter's fireside, smoking his pipe in company with John Bowden, Teddy Maroon expressed his belief that building lighthouses was about the hardest and the greatest work that man could undertake; that the men who did undertake such work ought not only to receive double pay while on duty, but also half pay for the remainder of their natural lives; that the thanks of the king, lords, and commons, inscribed on vellum, should be awarded to each man; and that gold medals should be struck commemorative of such great events,—all of which he said with great emphasis, discharging a sharp little puff of smoke between every two or three words, and winding up with a declaration that "them was his sentiments."

To all this old John Potter gravely nodded assent, and old Martha—being quite deaf to sound as well as reason—shook her head so decidedly that her cap quivered again.

John Bowden ventured to differ. He—firing off little cloudlets of smoke between words, in emulation of his friend—gave it as his opinion that "war was wuss," an opinion which he founded on the authority of his departed father, who had fought all through the Peninsular campaign, and who had been in the habit of entertaining his friends and family with such graphic accounts of storming breaches, bombarding fortresses, lopping off heads, arms, and legs, screwing bayonets into men's gizzards and livers, and otherwise agonising human frames, and demolishing human handiwork, that the hair of his auditors' heads would certainly have stood on end if that capillary proceeding had been at all possible.

But Teddy Maroon did not admit the force of his friend's arguments. He allowed, indeed, that war was a great work, inasmuch as it was a great evil, whereas lighthouse-building was a great blessing; and he contended, that while the first was a cause of unmitigated misery, and productive of nothing better than widows, orphans, and national debts, the second was the source of immense happiness, and of salvation to life, limb, and property.

To this John Bowden objected, and Teddy Maroon retorted, whereupon a war of words began, which speedily waged so hot that the pipes of both combatants went out, and old John Potter found it necessary to assume the part of peace-maker, in which, being himself a keen debater, he failed, and there is no saying what might have been the result of it if old Martha had not brought the action to a summary close by telling her visitors in shrill tones to "hold their noise." This they did after laughing heartily at the old woman's fierce expression of countenance.

Before parting, however, they all agreed without deciding the question at issue—that lighthouse-building was truly a noble work.

Chapter Ten.

The Campaign of 1758.

The contrast was pleasant; repose after toil,—for stone-cutting in the yard on shore was rest compared with the labour at the Rock. Steady, regular, quiet progress; stone after stone added to the great pile, tested and ready for shipment at the appointed time. The commander-in-chief planning, experimenting, superintending. The men busy as bees; and, last but not least, delightful evenings with friends, and recountings of the incidents of the war. Such is the record of the winter.

The spring of 1758 came; summer advanced. The builders assumed the offensive, and sent out skirmishers to the Rock, where they found that the enemy had taken little or no rest during the winter, and were as hard at it as ever. Little damage, however, had been done.

The attacking party suffered some defeats at the outset. They found that their buoy was lost, and the mooring chain of the *Buss* had sunk during the winter. It was fished up, however, but apparently might as well have been let lie, for it could not hold the *Buss*, which broke loose during a gale, and had to run for Plymouth Sound. Again, on 3rd June; another buoy was lost, and bad weather continued till July. Then, however, a general and vigorous assault was made, the result being "great progress," so that, on the 8th of August, a noteworthy point was reached.

On that day the fourteenth "course" was laid, and this completed the "solid" part of the lighthouse. It rose 35 feet above the foundation.

From this point the true *house* may be said to have commenced, for, just above this course, the opening for the door was left, and the little space in the centre for the spiral staircase which was to lead to the first room.

As if to mark their disapproval of this event, the angry winds and waves, during the same month, raised an unusually furious commotion while one of the yawls went into the "Gut" or pool, which served as a kind of harbour, to aid one of the stone boats.

"She won't get out o' that *this* night," said John Bowden, alluding to the yawl, as he stood on the top of the "solid" where his comrades were busy working, "the wind's gettin' up from the east'ard."

"If she don't," replied one of the men, "we'll have to sleep where we are."

"Slape!" exclaimed Maroon, looking up from the great stone whose joints he had been carefully cementing, "it's little slape you'll do here, boys. Av we're not washed off entirely we'll have to howld on by our teeth and nails. It's a cowld look-out."

Teddy was right. The yawl being unable to get out of the Gut, the men in it were obliged to "lie on their oars" all night, and those on the top of the building, where there was scarcely shelter for a fly, felt both the "look-out" and the look-in so "cowld" that they worked all night as the only means of keeping themselves awake and comparatively warm. It was a trying situation; a hard night, as it were "in the trenches,"—but it was their first and last experience of the kind.

Thus foot by foot—often baffled, but never conquered—Smeaton and his men rose steadily above the waves until they reached a height of thirty-five feet from the foundation, and had got as far as the store-room (the first apartment) of the building. This was on the 2nd of October, on which day all the stones required for that season were put into this store-room; but on the 7th of the same month the enemy made a grand assault in force, and caused these energetic labourers to beat a retreat. It was then resolved that they should again retire into winter quarters. Everything on the Rock was therefore "made taut" and secure against the foe, and the workers returned to the shore, whence they beheld the waves beating against their tower with such fury that the sprays rose high above it.

The season could not close, however, without an exhibition of the peculiar aptitude of the *Buss* for disastrous action! On the 8th that inimitable vessel—styled by Teddy Maroon a "tub," and by the other men, variously, a "bumboat," a "puncheon," and a "brute" began to tug with tremendous violence at her cable.

"Ah then, darlin'," cried Maroon, apostrophising her, "av ye go on like that much longer it's snappin' yer cable ye'll be after."

"It wouldn't be the first time," growled John Bowden, as he leaned against the gale and watched with gravity of countenance a huge billow whose crest was blown off in sheets of spray as it came rolling towards them.

"Howld on!" cried Teddy Maroon, in anxiety.

If his order was meant for the *Buss* it was flatly disobeyed, for that charming example of naval architecture, presenting her bluff bows to the billow, snapt the cable and went quietly off to leeward!

"All hands ahoy!" roared William Smart as he rushed to the foresail halyards.

The summons was not needed. All the men were present, and each knew exactly what to do in the circumstances. But what avails the strength and capacity of man when his weapon is useless?

"She'll *never* beat into Plymouth Sound wi' the wind in this direction," observed one of the masons, when sail had been set.

"Beat!" exclaimed another contemptuously, "she can't beat with the wind in *any* direction."

"An' yit, boys," cried Maroon, "she may be said to be a first-rate baiter, for she always baits *us* complaitly."

"I never, no I never did see such a scow!" said John Bowden, with a deepening growl of indignation, "she's more like an Irish pig than a—"

"Ah then, don't be hard upon the poor pigs of owld Ireland," interrupted Maroon, pathetically.

"Bah!" continued Bowden, "I only wish we had the man that planned her on board, that we might keel-haul him. I've sailed in a'most every kind of craft that floats—from a Chinese junk to a British three-decker, and between the two extremes there's a pretty extensive choice of washin'-tubs, but the equal o' this here *Buss* I never did see—no never;

take another haul on the foretops'l halyards, boys, and shut your potato-traps for fear the wind blows your teeth overboard. Look alive!"

That the *Buss* deserved the character so emphatically given to her was proved by the fact that, after an unsuccessful attempt to reach the Sound, she was finally run into Dartmouth Roads, and, shortly afterwards, her ungainly tossings, for that season, came to a close.

Chapter Eleven.

The Last Campaign—and Victory!

The campaign of 1759 opened on the 3rd of July with an attack commanded by Smeaton in person in the old *Buss*.

Previous to this, on March 21st, the coast was visited by a gale of such severity that immense mischief was done on shore. Ships in the port, houses, etcetera, at Plymouth, were greatly damaged; nevertheless, the unfinished tower out upon the exposed Eddystone reef stood fast, having defied the utmost fury of winds and waves.

It was found, however, that some loss had been sustained, the buoy of the mooring chain, as usual, was gone; but worse than that, one of the stones left in the store-room, a mass which weighed four and a half hundredweight, was missing. It had been washed out of the store-room entry by the water!

This was a serious loss, as it obliged the men to retire to the *Buss*, where they were constrained to spin yarns and twirl their thumbs in idleness till the lost stone was replaced by another. Then they went to work according to custom "with a will," and, on the 21st of July, completed the second floor; a whole room with a vaulted roof having been built in seven days.

At this point they proceeded to fit in the entry and store-room doors; and here another vexatious check appeared imminent. It was found that the block-tin with which the door-hooks were to be fastened had been forgotten!

Doubtless Mr Smeaton felt inclined to emulate the weather by "storming" on this occasion, but that would have been of no use. Neither was it of any avail that Teddy Maroon scratched his head and wrinkled his visage like that of a chimpanzee monkey. The tin *was* not; the hooks would not hold without it, and to send ashore for it would have involved great delay. Mr Smeaton proved equal to the occasion.

"Off with you, lads, to the *Buss*," he cried, "and bring hither every pewter plate and dish on board."

"Think o' that now!" exclaimed Maroon his wrinkles expanding into a bland smile of admiration.

"Don't think of it, but *do* it," returned Smeaton, with a laugh.

The thing was done at once. The "plate" of the *Buss* was melted down and mixed with lead, the hooks were fixed into the jambs, and the doors were hung in triumph. Solid doors they were too; not slender things with wooden panels, but thick iron-plated affairs somewhat resembling the armour of a modern ship-of-war, and fitted to defy the ocean's most powerful battering-rams.

Progress thereafter was steady and rapid. There were points here and there in the work which served as landmarks. On the 6th of August Smeaton witnessed a strange sight—a bright halo round the top of the building. It was no miracle, though it looked like one. Doubtless some scientific men could give a satisfactory explanation of it, and prove that it was no direct interposition of the hand of God. So could they give a satisfactory account of the rainbow, though the rainbow *is* a direct sign to man. Whatever the cause, there the glory circled like a sign of blessing on the work, and a fitting emblem of the life-giving, because death-warding, beams which were soon to be sent streaming from that tower by the hand of man.

Three days afterwards they began to lay the balcony floor; on the 17th the main column was completed, and on the 26th the masonry was finished. It only remained that the lantern should be set up. But this lantern was a mighty mass of metal and glass, made with great care, and of immense strength and weight. Of course it had to be taken off to the rock in pieces, and we may almost say *of course* the ocean offered opposition. Then, as if everything had conspired to test the endurance and perseverance of the builders, the first and second coppersmiths fell ill on the 4th September. Skilled labour such as theirs could not readily be replaced in the circumstances, and every hour of the now far advanced season had become precious. Smeaton had set his heart on "showing a light" that year. In this difficulty, being a skilled mechanic himself, he threw off his coat and set to work with the men.

The materials of the lantern were landed on the 16th and fitted together, and the cupola was hoisted to its place on the 17th. This latter operation was extremely hazardous, the cupola being upwards of half a ton in weight, and it had to be raised outside the building and kept carefully clear of it the while. It seemed as if the elements themselves favoured this critical operation, or rather, as though they stood aghast and breathlessly still, while this, the crowning evidence of their defeat, was being put on. It was accomplished in less than half an hour, and, strange to say, no sooner was the tackling loosed and the screws that held the cupola fixed, than up got wind and sea once more in an uproarious gale of consternation from the east!

On the 18th a huge gilt ball was screwed on the top by Smeaton's own hand, and thus the building of the Eddystone lighthouse was finished.

There still remained, however, a good deal of copper and wood-work to be done in the interior, but there was now no doubt in Smeaton's mind that the light would be exhibited that season. He therefore removed his bed and stores from the *Buss* to the lighthouse, and remained there, the better to superintend the completion of the work.

One evening he looked into the upper storeroom, where some bars were being heated over a charcoal fire. He became giddy with the fumes, staggered, and fell down insensible. Assuredly poor Smeaton's labours would have terminated then and there if it had not been that one of the men had providentially followed him. A startled cry was heard—one of those cries full of meaning which cause men to leap half involuntarily to the rescue.

"Och! somebody's kilt," cried Maroon, flinging away his pipe and springing up the staircase, followed by others, "wather! wather! look alive there!"

Some bore Smeaton to the room below, and others ran down for sea-water, which they dashed over their master unmercifully. Whether or not it was the best treatment we cannot say, but it sufficed, for Smeaton soon recovered consciousness and found himself lying like a half drowned rat on the stone floor.

At last, on the 1st of October, the lantern was lighted for trial during the day, with 24 candles. They burned well though a gale was blowing. On the 4th an express was sent to the Corporation of the Trinity House to say that all was ready. A short delay was made to allow of the lighting-up being advertised, and finally, on the 16th of October 1759, the new Eddystone lighthouse cast its first benignant rays over the troubled sea.

It chanced on that day that an appropriate storm raged, as if to inaugurate the great event. Owing to this, Smeaton could not get off to be at the lighting-up of his own building. From the shore, however, he beheld its initiative gleam as it opened its bright eye to the reality of its grand position, and we can well believe that his hardy, persevering spirit exulted that night over the success of his labours. We can well believe, also, that there was in him a deeper and higher feeling than that of mere joy, if we may judge of the cast of his mind by the inscriptions put by him upon his work during progress and at completion.

Round the upper store-room, on the course under the ceiling, he chiselled the words:—

"Except the Lord build the house, they labour in vain that build it."

And on the last stone set, over the door of the lantern, was carved:—

"Praise God!"

The lighthouse, thus happily completed, rose to a height of seventy feet, and consisted of forty-six courses of masonry. The internal arrangements will be understood at once by reference to our engraving, which exhibits a section of the tower. There was first the solid part, 35 feet in height and 16 feet 8 inches in diameter at the top, the base being much wider. Then came the still very solid portion with the entrance-door and the spiral staircase. Above that, the first store-room, which had no windows. Next, the second store-room, with two windows. Next the kitchen, followed by the bed-room, both of which had four windows; and, last, the lantern. The rooms were 12 feet 4 inches in diameter, with walls 2 feet 2 inches thick, and the whole fabric, from top to bottom, was so dovetailed, trenailed, cemented, inter-connected, and bound together, that it formed and still continues, a unique and immoveable mass of masonry.

There were others besides Smeaton who watched, that night, with deep interest the opening of the Eddystone's bright eye.

In a humble apartment in the village of Cawsand Bay an aged man stood, supported by an elderly man, at a window, gazing seaward with an expression of intense expectation, while a very aged woman sat crooning over the fire, holding the hand of a fair girl just verging on early womanhood.

"D'ee see it yet, Tommy?" asked the old man, eagerly.

"No, not yet," replied Tommy, "not—yes—there—!"

"Ah! that's it, I see it," cried old John Potter, with a faint gleam of his old enthusiasm. "There it goes, brighter than ever. A blessed light, and much wanted, Tommy, much, much wanted."

He leaned heavily on his son's arm and, after gazing for some time, asked to be taken back to his chair opposite old Martha.

"What is it?" inquired Martha, bending her ear towards a pretty little mouth.

"Grandfather has just seen the new Eddystone lighted up for the first time," replied Nora.

"Ay, ay," said Martha in a moralising tone, as she turned her eyes towards the fire, "ay, ay, so soon! I always had a settled conviction that that lighthouse would be burnt."

"It's *not* burnt, grannie," said Nora, smiling, "it's only lighted up."

"Well, well, my dear," returned Martha, with a solemn shake of the head, "there an't much difference atween lighted-up an' burnt-up. It's just as I always said to your father, my dear—to your grandfather I mean—depend upon it, John, I used to say, that light'ouse will either be burnt up or blowed over. Ay, ay, dear me!"

She subsided into silent meditation, and thus, good reader, we shall bid her farewell, merely remarking that she and her honest husband did not die for a considerable time after that. As she grew older and blinder, old Martha became more and more attached to the Bible and the dictionary, as well as to dear good blooming Nora, who assisted her in the perusal of the former, her sweet ringing voice being the only one at last that the old woman could hear. But although it was evident that Martha had changed in many ways, her opinions remained immoveable. She feebly maintained these, and held her "settled convictions" to the last gasp.

As for Teddy Maroon, he returned to Ireland after the lighthouse was finished and quietly got married, and settled on the margin of the bog where the Teddy from whom he sprang still lingered, among his numerous descendants, the life of his juvenile kindred, and an oracle on lighthouses.

Time with its relentless scythe at last swept all the actors in our tale away: Generations after them came and went. The world grew older and more learned; whether more wise is still an open question! Knowledge increased, science and art advanced apace. Electricity, steam, iron, gold, muscle, and brain, all but wrought miracles, and almost everything underwent change more or less; but, amid all the turmoil of the world's progress and all the storms of elemental strife, one object remained unaltered, and apparently unalterable—the Eddystone Lighthouse! True, indeed, its lantern underwent vast improvements, the Argand lamp and lens replacing the old candle, and causing its crown to shine with a whiter light and an intensified glory as it grew older, but as regards its sturdy frame, there it has stood on the rugged rocks amid the tormented surges, presenting its bold and battered, but undamaged, front to the utmost fury of blast and billow for upwards of a hundred years.

Printed in Great Britain
by Amazon.co.uk, Ltd.,
Marston Gate.